The Science of Elections

The Editors of *Scientific American*

SCIENTIFIC AMERICAN | **EDUCATIONAL PUBLISHING**

New York

Published in 2025 by Scientific American Educational Publishing
in association with **The Rosen Publishing Group**
2544 Clinton Street, Buffalo NY 14224

Contains material from Scientific American®, a division of Springer Nature America, Inc.,
reprinted by permission, as well as original material from The Rosen Publishing Group®.

First Edition

Scientific American
Lisa Pallatroni: Project Editor

Rosen Publishing
Michael Hessel-Mial: Compiling Editor
Michael Moy: Senior Graphic Designer

Cataloging-in-Publication Data
Names: Scientific American, Inc.
Title: The science of elections / edited by the Scientific American Editors.
Description: First Edition. | New York : Scientific American Educational Publishing, 2025. |
Series: Scientific American explores big ideas | Includes bibliographical references and index.
Identifiers: ISBN 9781725351684 (pbk.) | ISBN 9781725351691
(library bound) | ISBN 9781725351707 (ebook)
Subjects: LCSH: Presidents–United States–Election–Juvenile literature. |
Elections–United States–Juvenile literature. | Electoral college–United States-
-Juvenile literature. | Voting–United States–Juvenile literature.
Classification: LCC JK528.S356 2025 | DDC 324.973–dc23

Manufactured in the United States of America
Websites listed were live at the time of publication.

Cover: Rawpixel.com/Shutterstock.com

CPSIA Compliance Information: Batch # CSSA25.
For Further Information contact Rosen Publishing at 1-800-237-9932.

CONTENTS

INTRODUCTION

For all the frustrations people have with their elected leaders and the political process that selects them, it's easy to forget the basic principle of democracy: that people have a say in how their lives are governed. In a time when people feel those frustrations very acutely, it's especially useful to turn to the insights of science into how our democracies work. After all, many of the challenges of democracy (partisanship, misinformation, quirks or poor design in voting systems) have been widely researched and can be better understood. With that understanding, democracy can be improved if we demand it.

The articles in this title showcase different ways science can inform the political process. The first section is about the systems we use to vote, ranging from ballot design to interesting voting methods not yet widely used in the United States. The second section explores opinion polling, a complex science requiring mastery of statistics. In this section we learn more about challenges gauging public opinion, especially useful following two presidential election cycles with significant polling error. The third section focuses on psychological questions: What is the profile of most effective politicians? What motivates us as voters? What happens in our brains when we disagree? The fourth section covers varying threats to democracy. Some of these include attacks on voting systems from outside the country, but others highlight how partisan control of voting systems can deprive people of their rights. The final section is about when science and policy meet. In these articles, the writers and editors of *Scientific American* warn us about the damage that can be done by politicians who don't believe in science.

For democracy to work, citizens must not only share their input, but stay engaged to ensure that the voting process is always improving. Armed with the information in this title, you yourself can help keep that process going.

Section 1: Voting Systems

The Problems with Poor Ballot Design

By Catherine Caruso

Tensions are mounting as we hurtle towards Election Day this Tuesday, yet with all the focus on who's voting and where, most of us have put little thought into another essential part of the election process: the voting ballot itself. There are significant issues with the mechanics of voting, including the design of ballots and instructions for using them. Philip Kortum is a psychology professor at Rice University who studies how people interact with voting systems in real-world settings. He and Michael Byrne, also at Rice, recently co-authored a paper in *Current Directions in Psychological Science* that delves into the many issues that can arise during the voting process when poorly designed ballot systems trick people into voting incorrectly—or not at all. Here he answers some questions from contributor Catherine Caruso about what can go wrong. An edited transcript of the interview follows.

Q: What are the main types of balloting problems you encountered during your research?

A: There are four general classes of major voting issues we see with balloting. We've got ballot design issues in candidate voting, we've got instructional issues (issues relating to how officials tell people how to vote), we've got issues related to language on the ballot, and then there is just the way people interact with voting systems in general.

Q: Can you provide some examples of these issues?

A: When we talk about interface issues associated with how the ballot is put together, I think the Florida butterfly ballot [in the 2000 presidential election] is the classic example, where the layout of the ballot itself caused people to make errors.

Ballot instructions are often mandated by state legislatures but are written by local election officials, so often they're either too confusing or too dense. They'll describe something that could be described simply by using lots of words, or they may not describe the situation in the same way the user would think of it.

We also talk about confusing ballot language. We see this quite frequently, where ballot initiatives are written in ways that don't really reflect the way the voting public might be thinking about it. We're going through an issue in Houston this year where we're talking about recapture of property taxes, and the balloting language is very, very confusing.

And then people may become overburdened with the technology or by the circumstances surrounding the voting situation. We talk about, for example, the problem of people completing their ballots and then walking away without pressing the "cast" button, or completing their paper ballot and then walking out of the balloting station with it. In electronic voting systems, the phenomenon is so common that it has a name—the "fleeing voter problem." Voters believe they're done, so they walk away, and the election officials are left to determine, should they press the cast button? Or maybe they don't see this and the next person comes into the voting booth—do they press the cast button?

Q: What other problems come up with electronic voting systems?

A: The way the technology is implemented can confuse people. Sometimes the devices look like they're touch screens but they're not, and so people try to interact with them in weird ways. Or the data entry device is unusual. There's a balloting system that uses a wheel that you turn to move through the different selections, and that's unusual, you don't see wheel interfaces on most computers. Over the last couple of years, these systems have begun to reach the end of their service lives, and because of the many problems people have encountered with them, many jurisdictions are now transitioning back to some form of paper balloting.

Q: **What do you think are the biggest challenges to creating ballots that are well designed?**

A: I think we've got two sets of problems. One is that the system is completely decentralized. The states are the ones who set the foundational rules for the elections, but every county creates its own ballots and its own rules about how it's going to conduct elections. And so. we've got thousands of jurisdictions creating their own ballots, and the election officials are doing their absolute best, but they're not trained in psychological science, and so they may not understand all the issues that could arise.

I think the other issue is that it's not like you can create a ballot once and then say, Okay, this is perfect, and reuse it. You create a ballot, and then for the next election you have to create another ballot, and it may have different constraints, such as more races. So you're constantly changing the content of what you're presenting to users.

Q: **Are there a few overarching things that a good ballot does that makes it easy to understand and to use?**

A: Well, certainly a good ballot has instructions that are exceptionally clear and easy to read. If it's an electronic system, the navigation is very clear and allows voters to move around the interface quickly and easily. And the system will use color in appropriate ways to help voters understand what's happening. For example, if a voter failed to vote in a race, perhaps it would highlight that on the review screen using color. A lot of it is trying to create the greatest clarity in not only each of the races, but also in how voters move from race to race. And that's true even for paper ballots. You want each race to be clearly identified, labeled and segmented from the other races, so voters can easily move from section to section.

Q: **What are things that we can do as voters to make sure that we're voting successfully and not making any errors?**

A: One of the best things voters can do is to prepare. Many jurisdictions will provide sample ballots—you can go through and mark a sample ballot from the comfort and convenience of your home, so you have more time to work through it, and if you have any questions, you can seek that information out. Then, when you go to the polling station to cast your actual ballot, you'll be very well prepared—there won't be any surprises. I also think voters should be very careful about reviewing the final screen or checking their ballots to make sure that they're actually casting their vote as they intend.

Q: **Is there anything you encountered during your research that was particularly surprising or interesting?**

A: One of the things that always fascinates me is that people are often very quick to blame the voter, and say, I can't believe someone couldn't figure that out. But you have to remember that these are people who have made lots of conscious decisions to say, I want to participate in the democratic process, and so when they make these kinds of mistakes, it means that there's something about the system that is causing this to happen. Often it's the design.

Are Blockchains the Answer for Secure Elections? Probably Not

By Jesse Dunietz

With the U.S. heading into a pivotal midterm election, little progress has been made on ensuring the integrity of voting systems—a concern that retook the spotlight when the 2016 presidential election ushered Donald Trump into the White House amid allegations of foreign interference.

A raft of start-ups has been hawking what they see as a revolutionary solution: repurposing blockchains, best known as the digital transaction ledgers for cryptocurrencies like Bitcoin, to record votes. Backers say these internet-based systems would increase voter access to elections while improving tamper-resistance and public auditability. But experts in both cybersecurity and voting see blockchains as needlessly complicated, and no more secure than other online ballots.

Existing voting systems do leave plenty of room for suspicion: Voter impersonation is theoretically possible (although investigations have repeatedly found negligible rates for this in the U.S.); mail-in votes can be altered or stolen; election officials might count inaccurately; and nearly every electronic voting machine has proved hackable. Not surprisingly, a Gallup poll published prior to the 2016 election found a third of Americans doubted votes would be tallied properly.

Chain Voting

Blockchain advocates say the technology addresses the root cause of voting systems' insecurity—the fact that voting can be controlled by a single person, group or machine. Argentina's "Net Party" provides an example of what can go wrong. The tiny political party fields candidates who promise to strictly follow citizens' bidding as expressed on an online polling platform. When its leaders were pondering interparty alliances in early 2014, they put the decision to a vote among party members. To their horror, they discovered database administrators were selectively delaying new voter registrations until after the referendum, skewing the participant pool toward the administrators' preferred outcome.

Shenanigans like this one are possible only when an official (or a small cabal thereof) can unilaterally decide which votes or voters make the cut. Inspired by this realization, Net Party founder Santiago Siri went on to found Democracy Earth, a blockchain voting start-up. Democracy Earth and its peers aim to prevent corruption by decentralizing the voting process, subjecting each decision and vote to the public review of a blockchain.

Functionally, a blockchain is simply a convoluted database. Each entry in Bitcoin's database, for example, is a transaction in a digital ledger. The ledger publicly lists all transactions to date, implicitly specifying who retains how much money. What distinguishes a blockchain from conventional databases is that it enables multiple parties to share a database without centralized control. Most conventional databases have one authoritative computer that governs the process of adding data. In a blockchain, that trusted gatekeeper is replaced by computers all over the internet, each maintaining its own copy of the database. These computers act as validators for new data: When Alice wants to send money to Bob, she broadcasts the transaction to the validators, which must confirm for themselves the transaction adheres to the blockchain's rules (for example, that Alice has not sent more bitcoins than she owns). Once a majority of the network has accepted the transactions, they become the de facto consensus history.

Although blockchains' most prominent uses are monetary, there is no reason they cannot store other types of data—and votes would seem an excellent fit. An ideal voting system resists corruption by authorities or hackers and empowers citizens and auditors to agree on an election's outcome. Conveniently, auditable consensus among parties who do not fully trust one another is exactly what blockchains offer.

Each of the companies buying into this vision brings its own flavor. One start-up called Votem built its systems around academic research on letting voters check that individual votes were counted. Voatz, another start-up, supplements the blockchain with biometric identity verification, using smartphones' and tablets' built-in fingerprint readers and facial recognition to authenticate voters. Democracy Earth offers the ability to delegate your vote to another voter whose judgment you trust. Smartmatic, a prominent voting technology firm, integrates a blockchain into its broader suite of voting services. Products from these companies and others are attracting tentative interest from U.S. political parties, the U.S. military and governments including those of Brazil and Switzerland.

Details Full of Devils

Still, neither cryptographers nor election experts are impressed with blockchains' potential to improve election integrity. Noted cryptographer Ron Rivest of the Massachusetts Institute of Technology sums up the bleak consensus among academics: "I don't know of any who think it's a good idea, and within one or two years I expect all these companies to die."

Blockchain voting would require more than simply replacing Bitcoin transactions with votes. "Bitcoin works because you don't need [centrally issued] identities," says Arthur Gervais, a blockchain researcher at University College London. Instead, users generate public "addresses," which act like deposit-only account numbers for receiving money, along with secret digital "keys" that are needed to transfer money out of the corresponding accounts. Anyone can create key-address pairs willy-nilly. The catch: there is no recourse if you lose your secret key or leak it to a thief, in which case your address might as well contain the ashes of dollar bills.

This situation will not fly for government elections, where state and local authorities manage lists of eligible voters. Neither would most governments tolerate the possibility of a voter being disenfranchised if their digital voting key is swallowed by a damaged hard drive or stolen by a thief to cast a fraudulent vote.

This is why most blockchain election providers partially centralize the management of voter identities. Their systems are designed to query a consortium of several different identity databases such as government-issued IDs and fingerprints collected during registration to match the voter with a name from government voter polls. A quorum of these identity authorities can also revoke lost or stolen voting keys. Similarly, the companies partially centralize the validation process to guard against malicious influence: Instead of allowing anyone to become a validator, the government or party organizing the election designates a consortium of universities, nongovernmental organizations and such whose consensus determines what makes it onto the blockchain.

Unlike a Bitcoin-style open model, this consortium-managed blockchain model is at least implementable without damaging the election process, says Joe Kiniry, CEO of elections security company Free & Fair and principal scientist at Galois, a software company specializing in trustworthy software. But switching to a consortium also wipes out the blockchain's supposed security benefits. Having voter identities dispensed and revoked by central authorities puts voters back at the mercy of a few administrators who can decide which votes count. The role of validators, meanwhile, is reduced to auditing for fraudulent votes, which can be achieved far more simply. "Blockchains are a very interesting and useful technology for distributed consensus where there is no central authority. But elections just don't fit that model," says Microsoft senior cryptographer Josh Benaloh. Once a central entity is coordinating an election, "you might as well have that entity publish [vote] data on [a Web site], digitally sign it and be done."

In fact, Kiniry and Gervais both contend blockchain technology does not even solve the core problems of online election integrity. "If you look at all the technology components necessary," Kiniry says, a blockchain "only ticks, like, the first four boxes out of a hundred." It works for recording votes, but even blockchain start-ups need additional layers of technology for thornier challenges such as validating voters, keeping ballots secret and letting each voter verify their vote was tallied.

Cryptographers have spent decades advocating for their preferred solutions to those challenges—a suite of techniques known as "end-to-end verifiable voting." These techniques make no use of blockchains; in fact, Benaloh says they solve all the problems a blockchain does and then some. Ironically, though, helping end-to-end verifiability go mainstream might end up being blockchains' greatest contribution to election security. After all, the word "blockchain" draws investor cash even to companies whose connection to the technology is, speaking generously, tenuous. And even skeptics acknowledge blockchains' relevance to voting; despite their questionable utility for security, similar procedures can enhance voting systems' efficiency or reliability. So someone may well find a way to build a cryptographer-approved system and call it a blockchain. What if that's what it takes for end-to-end verifiability to get traction? "If that's what makes you adopt it, okay, let's do it," Benaloh says. "But I want to talk about all the real benefits of a good protocol as well."

About the Author

Jesse Dunietz is a computer scientist and the Technology, Energy, and Society Fellow at Securing America's Future Energy (SAFE).

The Vulnerabilities of Our Voting Machines

By Jen Schwartz

A few weeks ago computer scientist J. Alex Halderman rolled an electronic voting machine onto a Massachusetts Institute of Technology stage and demonstrated how simple it is to hack an election.

In a mock contest between George Washington and Benedict Arnold three volunteers each voted for Washington. But Halderman, whose research involves testing the security of election systems, had tampered with the ballot programming, infecting the machine's memory card with malicious software. When he printed out the results, the receipt showed Arnold had won, 2 to 1. Without a paper trail of each vote, neither the voters nor a human auditor could check for discrepancies. In real elections, too, about 20 percent of voters nationally still cast electronic ballots only.

As the U.S. midterm elections approach, Halderman, among others, has warned our "outmoded and under-tested" electronic voting systems are increasingly vulnerable to attacks. They can also lead to confusion. Some early voters in Texas have already reported votes they cast for Democratic U.S. Senate challenger Beto O'Rourke were switched on-screen to incumbent Republican Sen. Ted Cruz. There's no evidence of hacking, and the particular machines in question are known to have software bugs, which could account for the errors.

Halderman does not think an attack is to blame. "If it was, the candidate switch wouldn't be visible to either the voter nor election officials," he says. "But what's happening in Texas is another warning sign of aging machines not functioning well, which makes them fertile ground for vote-stealing attacks."

Ultimately—whether scenarios like the one in Texas stem from glitchy software, defective machinery or an adversarial hack—one outcome is a loss of confidence in our election process. And as cybersecurity journalist Kim Zetter recently wrote in *The New York Times Magazine*, "It's not too grand to say that if there's a failure in the ballot box, then democracy fails."

Halderman, who directs the University of Michigan Center for Computing and Society, recently spoke with *Scientific American* about the different types of technological threats to democracy—and how good old-fashioned paper can safeguard elections.

[An edited transcript of the interview follows:]

Q: It seems like election interference is occurring all around us, in so many different ways. How is the hacking of voting-machine software related to the disinformation campaigns that show up in our Facebook feeds?

A: Technology is transforming democracy on a lot of different levels, and they're not entirely connected. But they all create vulnerabilities in the way that society forms political opinions, expresses those opinions and translates them into election results.

One form of Russian meddling in the 2016 election, for example, was social media campaigns, which affect political discourse at the level of opinions formed by individuals. But the second prong—the hacking into campaigns, like John Podesta's e-mail—was just so sinister in the way it was picking only on one side. That gets to the very roots of how open societies traditionally rely on information gathering and the media in order to make sound political decisions.

And then there's the third form of hacking: going after the machinery of elections, the infrastructure, polling places, voter registration systems, etcetera. That's where most of my work has been.

Q: How did you end up investigating voting security?

A: It was literally dropped into my lap while I was in grad school at Princeton in 2006. No research group had ever had access to a U.S. voting machine in order to do a security analysis, and an anonymous group offered to give us one to study. Back then there was quite a dispute between researchers who hypothesized there would be vulnerabilities in polling place equipment and the manufacturers that insisted everything was fine.

Q: Over the past decade, how has the field of election cybersecurity changed?

A: It has moved away from a position of hubris. Now that there have been major academic studies there is scientific consensus that here *will* be vulnerabilities in polling place equipment.

Sometimes the risks or probable failure modes of new technology are totally foreseeable. And that was certainly the case in voting. As paperless computer voting machines were being introduced, there were many computer scientists who—before anyone had even studied one of these machines directly—were saying, "This just isn't a good idea to have elections be conducted by, essentially, black box technology."

On the other hand, the ways in which these failures will be exploited—and the implications of that exploitation—are sometimes a bit harder to foresee. When we did the first voting machine study 10 years ago, we talked about a range of different possible attackers, dishonest election officials and corrupt candidates. But the notion that it would be a foreign government cyber attack, that that would be one of the biggest problems to worry about—well, that was pretty far down on the list. Over the past 10 years cyber warfare went from something that seemed like science fiction to something you read about every almost every day in the newspaper.

2016 really did change everything. It taught us that our threat models were wrong. I think it caught much of the intelligence community off guard, and it caught much of the cybersecurity community off guard. It was surreal to see Russia get so close to actually exploiting the vulnerabilities to harm us.

Q: The Department of Homeland Security and intelligence community say there's no evidence that Russian hackers

altered votes in the 2016 presidential election. Can you put "no evidence" in context?

A: We know for sure that in 2016 the Russians didn't do everything that they are capable of. Most of the evidence—both of Russian attack and of Russian restraint—is in the context of voter-registration systems, which are another back-end system operated by each state.

If you read carefully the statements of the intelligence communities, our evidence that no votes were changed is that we apparently didn't hear particular Russian operatives who were responsible for *other* parts of the attack planning or attempting a vote-manipulation attack. But that's not very reassuring, because we don't know what other attackers might have been attempting, for which we might not have the same level of intelligence insight. It's hard to know what you don't know. There are other adversaries who certainly benefit from manipulating American elections, including other countries like China or North Korea.

The voting machines themselves have received much, much, much less scrutiny post-2016 from intelligence and defensive sides—as far as we know in the public sphere anyway. To my knowledge, no state has done any kind of rigorous forensics on their voting machines to see whether they had been compromised.

Q: So potentially there's more going on that's not being looked at as closely?

A: That's right. But what we do know from the Senate Intelligence Committee's report, based on its investigation of the Russian election interference, was that Russia was in a position to do more damage than they did to the registration systems. They were in a position to modify or destroy data in at least some states' registration systems, which if it had gone undetected, would have caused massive chaos on Election Day. But they decided not to pull the trigger.

Q: **When it comes to voting machines themselves, though, how might malicious code get introduced?**

A: One possibility is that attackers could infiltrate what are called election-management systems. These are small networks of computers operated by the state or the county government or sometimes an outside vendor where the ballot design is prepared.

There's a programming process by which the design of the ballot—the races and candidates, and the rules for counting the votes—gets produced, and then gets copied to every individual voting machine. Election officials usually copy it on memory cards or USB sticks for the election machines. That provides a route by which malicious code could spread from the centralized programming system to many voting machines in the field. Then the attack code runs on the individual voting machines, and it's just another piece of software. It has access to all of the same data that the voting machine does, including all of the electronic records of people's votes.

So how do you infiltrate the company or state agency that programs the ballot design? You can infiltrate their computers, which are connected to the internet. Then you can spread malicious code to voting machines over a very large area. It creates a tremendously concentrated target for attack.

Q: **Where does this leave us heading into the midterms?**

A: Although there's greatly increased security awareness (and increased protection for registration systems in particular) compared to 2016, there are so many gaps left in election security—particularly when it comes to polling place equipment. It would certainly be possible to sabotage election systems in ways that would cause massive chaos. If nothing happens this November, it's going to be because our adversaries chose not to pull the trigger. Not because they had no way of doing us harm.

Q: **What if an adversary's goal isn't widespread chaos, but something subtler?**

A: Unfortunately, it's also possible to more subtly manipulate things, especially in close elections, in ways that would result in the wrong candidates winning—and with high probability of that not being detected.

Q: I'm thinking about close races for the Senate and the House, such as in Texas and in Georgia.

A: The broader question is if we're going to have a tight national contest for control of Congress, it's going to hinge on a set of swing districts. Because our election system is so distributed, with localities and states making their own critical security decisions, it means some are going to be much weaker than others. And sophisticated adversaries like Russia could try to probe the election security across all of those likely swing districts, find the ones that are most weakly protected and subtly manipulate results in those districts. And if they can do it in enough swing districts, they can flip the outcome—and control of Congress. That's what's so scary.

Q: The National Academies of Sciences, Engineering and Medicine released a report in September that urged all states to adopt paper ballots before 2020. Why is paper best for verifying election outcomes?

A: The idea of a post-election paper audit is a form of quality control. You want to have people inspect enough of the paper records to confirm with high statistical probability that the outcome on the paper and the outcome on the electronic results is the same. You're basically doing a random sample. How large a sample you need depends on how close the election result was. If it was a landslide, a very small sample—maybe even just a few hundred random ballots selected from across the state—could be enough to confirm with high statistical confidence that it was indeed a landslide. But if the election result was a tie, well, you need to inspect every ballot to confirm that it was a tie.

The key insight behind auditing as a cyber defense is that if you have a paper record that the voter got to inspect, then that can't later be changed by a cyber attack. The cost to do so is relatively low. My estimate is it would cost about $25 million a year to audit to high confidence every federal race nationally.

Q: **But this strategy is a problem for states like New Jersey and Georgia, where currently there's no paper trail at all.**

A: Today only about 79 percent of votes across the country are recorded on a piece of paper. If you have no paper trail, then it's impossible to perform a rigorous audit. At best you're just hitting the print button again on a computer program. You're going to get the same result you got the first time, whether it is true or not.

There are about 14 specific states that have gaps where ballots aren't being recorded on paper, and that's known to everyone. Georgia, for example, is entirely paperless. And they are also using voting machines with software that hasn't [had a security patch] since 2005.

Q: **What are you most concerned about in the 2018 midterm elections?**

A: That it's too late to do anything else. Except for maybe some states to tighten up their postelection procedures.

The focus needs to start being on 2020. Because it's going to take that long for some states to replace their aging and vulnerable voting machines, and to make sure that every state has rigorous postelection audits in place. We have an opportunity to solve this problem. It's one of the few grand cybersecurity challenges that doesn't have to be difficult or expensive.

But it's going to take national leadership and national standards to get there. Otherwise we're not going to be able to move fast enough or in a coordinated manner, and the attackers that have us in their sights are going to win.

About the Author

Jen Schwartz is a senior features editor at Scientific American *since 2017. She produces stories and special projects about how society is adapting—or not—to a rapidly changing world, particularly in the contexts of climate change, health, and misinformation. Jen has led several editorial projects at* Scientific American, *including a special issue, "How Covid Changed The World" (March 2022); the "Confronting Misinformation" special report (November 2020); and "The Future of Money" special report (January 2018), for which she was interviewed in over a dozen media outlets including CNBC, CBS and WNYC. She's co-led projects including the "Truth, Lies, and Uncertainty" special issue (2019) and "Inconceivable" (2018) about research gaps in female reproductive health. Jen also writes and edits essays and book reviews for* Scientific American. *For 15 years, Jen has reported on sea-level rise and the vexing choices of coastal communities. In 2016, she flew with NASA's Operation Icebridge over Antarctica to report on how polar observations of ice melt lead to ever-improving models for sea-level rise; her resulting feature story, about how a community in NJ is retreating from worsening floods, won the 2019 "Science in Society Award" from the National Association of Science Writers. It has been widely cited in policy and academia, and she has discussed her work on radical climate adaptation at places including the World Economic Forum's Sustainable Development Summit, Telluride Mountainfilm festival, PBS's Story in The Public Square, The Denver Museum of Natural History, and Princeton University's Council on Science and Technology. Jen has moderated panel discussions for a range of audiences, from corporate (3M's State of The World's Science), to global development (UN General Assembly), to government (Earth From Space Institute) to the arts (Tribeca Film Festival). Jen previously worked at* Popular Science, GQ, New York Magazine, Outside, *and* The Boston Globe. *She has a B.S. in journalism from the College of Communication at Boston University.*

How Medical Systems Can Help People Vote

By Ilan Shapiro, Shweta Namjoshi and Olivia S. Morris

Hospitals and community health centers are cornerstones of our communities. At our clinics at AltaMed Health Services in Los Angeles and Orange counties and Stanford Medicine in the San Francisco Bay Area, we treat hundreds of thousands of people per year, many of whom are young, disabled, low-income and/or people of color. Far too many of the people we serve are disengaged in democracy, and because policy at all levels of government shapes our health, this has to change.

Recognizing this need, a growing number of U.S. health care providers are making voter engagement a routine aspect of clinical care to reduce health inequity. More than 300 institutions and 30,000 providers have added nonpartisan civic health to their checklist of ways to care for the whole person, with the hope that helping people vote can address long-standing health disparities. Making ballots more available can help people better advocate for their health needs, not just in voting for people who campaign on health-related issues such as clean air, better access to health care, and women's or children's health, but also for the social determinants of health—affordable housing, food security, environmental justice and disability accommodation. These social determinants account for up to 80 percent of health outcomes, and are equally critical to promoting both individual and public health.

Health systems are well-positioned to address these inequities, and federal legislation empowers them to do so. The National Voter Registration Act of 1993 and guidance from the Internal Revenue Service support nonprofit organizations—like many hospitals and clinics—in nonpartisan voter registration.

AltaMed is one of many examples. In the run-up to the 2022 primaries in California, AltaMed staff and people from local civic engagement organizations reached more than 220,000 new and low-propensity Latino voters within a five-mile radius of all their clinic sites, despite usually low voter turnout in midterm compared with general elections. In 2018, as part of the AltaMed Get Out the Vote campaign, which involved hospital staff and our partner community health centers, we contacted nearly 30,000 Black and Latino voters in primarily Latino precincts. Every 1 percent of total voters contacted by AltaMed translated into an 8 percent increase in voter turnout between 2014 and 2018.

Individual health care providers are also bringing nonpartisan conversations about voting into their clinical practice. Professionals at more than 700 hospitals and clinics nationwide have helped both colleagues and their patients register to vote with tools from nonprofit partners like Vot-ER. They help people to register, without endorsing a political party, policy or candidate. The power then lies with the voter to choose who best represents them and use their own voice to advocate for their health.

The COVID pandemic exacerbated and highlighted how social determinants of health affect health outcomes, and it spurred health care–based efforts to increase voter turnout. In August 2020, nearly 100 health and democracy partners celebrated the first Civic Health Month to ensure that people could access voting resources and cast their ballots safely during the presidential election. This coalition has since grown to more than 300 partners, including the National Medical Association, a professional organization that represents physicians of African descent as well as people of African descent seeking medical care, Dana Farber Cancer Institute, American College of Obstetricians and Gynecologists, and the American Academy of Pediatrics. In addition, more than 80 medical schools participated in the Healthy Democracy Campaign, helping 15,692 people.

Vot-ER has reported that in 2020, institutions and providers used the organization's tools to help more than 47,000 people initiate voter registration or request a mail-in ballot. Of that number, 84 percent of people who completed the registration process did so successfully, and of those who registered successfully, 85 percent voted in the general election. More people of color and young people voted after registering through Vot-ER than in the general electorate.

Major voices in health care have also taken action. In June, the American Medical Association passed a resolution affirming voting as a social determinant of health. The U.S. Department of Health and Human Services reestablished voting as a research objective in Healthy People 2030, the framework used to measure and improve health outcomes. The Association of American Medical Colleges also issued guidance encouraging teaching hospitals and medical schools to support voter access in their communities.

At a time when U.S. life expectancy has hit the largest two-year decline in nearly a century, one of the most fundamental ways to ensure that policy improves health is to ensure people vote. Regardless of the candidates or offices up for election, our health is always on the ballot. From the national level to the individual health care worker, we need to continue taking action that underscores voting and health as part of the same conversation—one that encourages our colleagues and patients to advocate for themselves and to vote like our health depends on it, because it does.

This is an opinion and analysis article, and the views expressed by the author or authors are not necessarily those of Scientific American.

About the Authors

Ilan Shapiro is chief health correspondent and medical affairs officer for AltaMed Health Services, California's largest not-for-profit Federally Qualified Health Center.

Shweta Namjoshi is a pediatric gastroenterologist at Stanford Medicine and is assistant director of health policy with the Office of Child Health Equity. She speaks in this piece as an individual and not as a representative of her employer.

Olivia S. Morris is a recent graduate of Harvard College and a former intern at Vot-ER & Civic Health Month.

Citizens' Assemblies Are Upgrading Democracy: Fair Algorithms Are Part of the Program

By Ariel Procaccia

I n 1983 the Eighth Amendment to the Irish constitution enshrined an abortion ban that had prevailed in the nation for more than a century. Public opinion on the issue shifted in the new millennium, however, and by 2016 it was clear that a real debate could no longer be avoided. But even relatively progressive politicians had long steered clear of the controversy rather than risk alienating voters. Who would be trustworthy and persuasive enough to break the deadlock?

The answer was a bunch of ordinary people. Seriously. The Irish Parliament convened a citizens' assembly, whose 99 members were chosen at random. The selection process ensured that the group's composition represented the Irish population along dimensions such as age, gender and geography. Over several months in 2016 and 2017, the assembly heard expert opinions and held extensive discussions regarding the legalization of abortion. Its recommendation, supported by a significant majority of members, was to allow abortions in all circumstances, subject to limits on the length of pregnancy. These conclusions set the stage for a 2018 referendum in which 66 percent of Ireland's voters chose to repeal the Eighth Amendment, enabling abortion to be legalized. Such an outcome had been almost inconceivable a few years earlier.

The Irish citizens' assembly is just one example of a widespread phenomenon. In recent years hundreds of such groups have convened around the world, their members randomly selected from the concerned population and given time and information to aid their deliberations. Citizens' assemblies in France, Germany, the U.K., Washington State and elsewhere have charted pathways for reducing carbon emissions. An assembly in Canada sought methods of mitigating hate speech and fake news; another in Australia recommended ethical approaches to human genome editing; and yet another in Oregon identified policies for COVID pandemic recovery. Taken together, these assemblies have demonstrated an impressive capacity to uncover the will of the people and build consensus.

The effectiveness of citizens' assemblies isn't surprising. Have you ever noticed how politicians grow a spine the moment they decide not to run for reelection? Well, a citizens' assembly is a bit like a legislature whose members make a pact barring them from seeking another term in office. The randomly selected members are not beholden to party machinations or outside interests; they are free to speak their mind and vote their conscience.

What's more, unlike elected bodies, these assemblies are chosen to mirror the population, a property that political theorists refer to as descriptive representation. For example, a typical citizens' assembly has a roughly equal number of men and women (some also ensure nonbinary participation), whereas the average proportion of seats held by women in national parliaments worldwide was 26 percent in 2021—a marked increase from 12 percent in 1997 but still far from gender balance. Descriptive representation, in turn, lends legitimacy to the assembly: citizens seem to find decisions more acceptable when they are made by people like themselves.

As attractive as descriptive representation is, there are practical obstacles to realizing it while adhering to the principle of random selection. Overcoming these hurdles has been a passion of mine for the past few years. Using tools from mathematics and computer science, my collaborators and I developed an algorithm for the selection of citizens' assemblies that many practitioners around the world are using. Its story provides a glimpse into the future of democracy—and it begins a long time ago.

The Goddess of Chance

Citizens' assemblies are the latest incarnation of an idea called sortition, the random selection of representatives, that dates back to classical Athens. In the fifth century B.C.E. the city-state, whose patron deity was Athena, embraced sortition to such a degree that one might say it was de facto governed by Tyche, the goddess of chance. A large majority of its public officials were selected by lot from among citizens who volunteered to serve. These included most of the magistrates, who formed the executive branch, thousands of jurors, and the entire Council of 500, a deliberative body with a wide range of responsibilities.

The Athenians' respect for sortition is apparent in the ingenious design of their lottery machine, the kleroterion, which was used to select jurors. It's a stone slab with a grid of slots, arranged in 10 vertical columns, corresponding to the 10 Athenian tribes. Citizens who wished to serve as jurors presented their lottery ticket—bronze tokens with identifying information—to a magistrate, who inserted each tribe's tokens into the slots in the appropriate column. The magistrate also poured marbles of two contrasting colors—say, gold and white—through a funnel into a cylinder, where they lined up in random order.

Then, the magistrate used a mechanism to reveal the marbles one by one. If the first marble was gold, the 10 citizens whose tokens appeared in the top row were added to the jury; if it was white, they were all dismissed. And so on, down the column of marbles and the rows of citizens: gold meant in; white meant out. To select a jury of 30 citizens, for example, the magistrate would include three gold marbles in the mix. Because each gold marble picks precisely one citizen from each tribe, any jury selected in this way would necessarily have an equal number of members from each tribe. This passed for descriptive representation in a society that practiced slavery and excluded women from the political process.

As clever as a kleroterion is, the present-day selection process for citizens' assemblies is more complicated because our concept of descriptive representation is much more nuanced. A citizens' assembly is expected to reflect many demographic attributes of the population, not just one. Take Climate Assembly U.K., which the House of Commons commissioned in 2019 to discuss how the nation should reach its target of zero greenhouse gas emissions by the year

2050. Organizers selected the 110 members randomly while seeking to represent the populace according to seven criteria: gender, age, geographic region, education, ethnicity, rural or urban residence, and climate views. Consider the rural-or-urban criterion: in the U.K., about 80 percent of the population lives in urban areas, so out of the 110 seats, 88 seats (or 80 percent) were reserved for urbanites, and 22 seats (or 20 percent) were allocated to country dwellers. Quotas were calculated similarly for each of the other criteria.

As if this isn't complicated enough, organizers of citizens' assemblies often face the challenge that they can select members only from among volunteers, and the pool of willing candidates may look nothing like the population. Typically the organizers issue invitations by mail or phone to a large number of people, but only a fraction of invitees opt in. For example, the organizers of Climate Assembly U.K. sent invitation letters to 30,000 households and mustered 1,727 volunteers. Of the latter, 63 percent had attained the highest level of education (in the British system), whereas a mere 27 percent of Britons fell into that category. It should also come as no surprise that the distribution of climate views among volunteers was skewed, with those concerned about the issue being overrepresented, compared with the general population: it is a rare climate skeptic who relishes the opportunity to spend long weekends charting a course to zero emissions.

To summarize, we need a modern-day kleroterion that can select a citizens' assembly that is representative in terms of multiple criteria—and can do so starting from an unrepresentative pool of volunteers. Thankfully, we've progressed from stone slabs to computers, so this problem boils down to the design of the right algorithm.

Until recently, the prevalent approach relied on what computer scientists call a "greedy algorithm." This is a bit of misnomer because such an algorithm is really guilty of sloth rather than greed: It takes the action that seems best right now, without making an effort to understand what would work well in the long term. To select an assembly, a greedy algorithm adds volunteers one by one in a way that makes the most immediate progress toward filling the quotas.

For example, the algorithm might determine that, right now, the assembly is sorely missing individuals in the 30-to-44 age group, and among all volunteers in this age group, it would choose one at random to join the assembly. Next, it might identify a shortage of Londoners and select someone from that group.

The algorithm may make some bad choices and end up in a situation where it is unable to fill the quotas, but in that case, it can simply restart, and experience shows that it will eventually catch a lucky break. In fact, a particular greedy algorithm developed by a U.K.-based nonprofit, the Sortition Foundation, was used to select that country's climate assembly and many other consequential assemblies.

To Be Fair

It was an examination of the greedy algorithm that instigated my own work on the selection of citizens' assemblies, done in collaboration with Bailey Flanigan and Anupam Gupta, both at Carnegie Mellon University, Paul Gölz of Harvard University and Brett Hennig of the Sortition Foundation. We realized that, in the greedy algorithm's short-sighted pursuit of filling quotas, it may sacrifice another important goal: giving all volunteers a fair chance of serving on the assembly. Political theorists view fairness as key to achieving democratic ideals such as equality of opportunity. To be sure, some imbalance is inevitable: Because the objective is descriptive representation of the entire population, volunteers who belong to groups that are underrepresented in the pool are more likely to be selected than those in overrepresented groups. In practice, however, the greedy algorithm excludes some volunteers from the process, even when it is unnecessary.

To see how the greedy algorithm is unfair, we can revisit the selection process of Climate Assembly U.K. by simulating the different assemblies put together by the algorithm, each of which could, in principle, have been the actual one. It turns out that the algorithm selects some of the 1,727 volunteers with a minuscule probability of less than 0.03 percent, whereas it is possible to guarantee that even the least fortunate volunteer is chosen with a probability of at least 2.6 percent—86 times higher—while meeting the same quotas.

To create a fairer algorithm, my collaborators and I adopt a holistic approach. Instead of considering volunteers one at a time, we consider the entire ensemble of potential assemblies, each of which meets all the demographic quotas. Each candidate assembly is given a lottery ticket that specifies its probability of being selected as the actual assembly. The probabilities are determined later, in such a way that they add up to 100 percent, and there's only one winning ticket.

Imagine that each volunteer is given a copy of the lottery ticket of every assembly of which they are a member. The volunteer is selected if any of their lottery tickets wins; in other words, the probability that a volunteer is selected is the sum of probabilities associated with all the potential assemblies that include them. Of all possible lotteries, our algorithm seeks to construct the fairest one, in the sense that the selection probability of the volunteer who is least likely to be chosen is as high as possible.

Now all we need to do is to go over all potential assemblies and ... oh wait, the number of potential assemblies is beyond astronomical. A common way to illustrate "astronomical" is to compare the quantity in question with the number of atoms in the observable universe, estimated to be at most 10^{82}. But even that doesn't quite cut it: if you took every atom in the universe and replaced it with an entire universe, each with 10^{82} atoms, the total number of atoms you'd get is still much smaller than the number of ways to select the 110 members of Climate Assembly U.K. from the 1,727 volunteers (without quotas).

Fortunately, computational problems at this mind-boggling scale are routinely solved by machinery from the field of optimization. To apply these techniques, one must construct a mathematical model that includes an objective (in this case, maximizing fairness) and defines a set of possible solutions. The goal is to find the optimal (fairest) solution out of all possible solutions. In another example, when a navigation app such as Google Maps plans a trip from one location to another, it is solving an optimization problem wherein every feasible route is a possible solution and the objective is to find the shortest possible travel time. In a large city, the number of routes can be enormous, yet we take it for granted that our phones will comb through all these possible trips in seconds. The problem of finding the fairest lottery of the potential assemblies is a much harder problem, but it, too, can be conquered by the right combination of optimization tools.

Our algorithm was released as open source in 2020 and has since become a common method for selecting citizens' assemblies. It was initially adopted by our partners at the Sortition Foundation, who have used it to select, among others, Scotland's climate assembly, convened by the Scottish government; a citizens' jury on assisted dying in Jersey Island, which led to its parliament's decision to allow the practice in principle; and a public advisory group created by the U.K.'s National Health Service to discuss how the government should use data in its response to the COVID pandemic. Other organizations have employed our algorithm to select major citizens' assemblies in Germany, France and the U.S., including a panel in Michigan to chart a pathway for pandemic recovery. Last year, thanks to an effort led by Gölz and Gili Rusak, a doctoral student at Harvard, our algorithm became freely accessible through the website Panelot.org (panel selection by lot), making it even easier for practitioners to apply it.

The Democracy Code

An American time traveler visiting the present from the late 18th century would find an almost unrecognizable world, but one thing, at least, would look eerily familiar: the way our system of democracy works. Although the endurance of the political system is a tribute to the framers of the constitution, it's abundantly clear that not all is well. In America and in some other democracies around the world, faith in governments has hit rock bottom, and even the most popular legislation often fails to be enacted. There's an urgent need to rethink the practice of democracy using modern tools.

I believe that mathematicians and computer scientists have a significant role to play in this endeavor. We love to talk of "democratizing AI" or "democratizing finance," but democracy itself demands our attention. An algorithmic approach is crucial to the construction of new frameworks to engage citizens and give them a voice. But this apparatus of democracy comes with uniquely challenging instructions: "random assembly required."

About the Author

Ariel Procaccia is Gordon McKay Professor of Computer Science at Harvard University. He is an expert in algorithms and artificial intelligence and is especially interested in questions of societal importance.

Could Math Design the Perfect Electoral System?

By Jack Murtagh

Third-party presidential candidates are often blamed for ruining an election for one of the major political parties by "stealing" votes away from them. But with a little help from the math of social choice theory, elections could embrace the Ralph Naders of the world.

Take the historically tight Gore vs. Bush U.S. presidential election in 2000, when Americans anxiously awaited the resolution of legal battles and a recount that wouldn't reveal a winner for another month. At the time the *Onion* published the headline "Recount Reveals Nader Defeated." Of course Ralph Nader was never a serious contender for office. This led many to suggest that the Green Party candidate, like other third-party politicians, had attracted enough votes away from one of the two major parties to tip the scales against them (in this case the Democrats, who lost the election by just 537 votes).

Ranked choice voting is an alternative electoral system that would mitigate the spoiler effect while giving voters more voice to express themselves at the polls, social choice theorists suggest. Ranked choice voting boasts some obvious advantages. The mathematical discussion over how best to implement it, however, is surprisingly subtle. And an old theorem from economics suggests that *all* attempts to use ranked choice voting are vulnerable to counterintuitive results.

Rather than voting only for a single candidate, ranked choice voting allows people to rank the candidates in order of preference. This way, if somebody wanted to support Nader but didn't want to take away a vote from Gore, they could have ranked Gore second at the voting booth. When Nader didn't amass enough votes, the second place ranking for Gore would still benefit him in the election. Proponents also contend that ranked choice voting disincentivizes vicious mudslinging campaign tactics. That's because, unlike in typical elections, candidates in ranked choice races would need to appeal to all voters, even those who wouldn't give them a top spot on the ballot. Currently Maine and Alaska have instituted ranked choice voting for all state and federal elections, including presidential primaries, in which it's more likely for multiple candidates to appeal to the same voters.

Once voters have ranked candidates, how does that information get aggregated to reveal a single winner? The answer is not as straightforward as it might seem, and many schemes have been proposed. Let's explore three approaches to vote tallying: plurality, instant runoff and "Condorcet methods," each of which leads to unexpected behavior.

Unlike instant runoff and Condorcet methods, plurality is not actually a ranked choice voting scheme. In fact, it's the most common voting method in the U.S.: whoever gains the most first-choice votes wins the election. Plurality can come with unfavorable outcomes. In addition to the problem of third-party election spoilers, imagine if candidate A received 34 percent of the votes, and candidates B and C each received 33 percent. Candidate A would win the plurality even if they were the *last* choice of every other voter. So 66 percent of the population would have their last pick for president. Plurality wastes votes and ignores the full spectrum of voter preferences.

A better method (and the one used in American implementations of ranked choice voting as well as to select the best picture at the Oscars) is called instant runoff. If no candidate receives more than half of the first-choice votes, then the candidate with the fewest first-choice votes is removed from consideration and their votes get reallocated according to voters' next choices (e.g., if your ranking of three candidates was 1) B, 2) C, 3) A, and candidate C gets removed for having the fewest first-choice votes, then A will get bumped up in your ballot to fill C's gap: 1) B, 2) A). The process of removing the candidate with fewest first-choice votes repeats until one candidate has a majority. While instant runoff wastes fewer votes than plurality, it has drawbacks of its own. Bizarre situations can arise where your favorite candidate is more likely to *lose* if they get *more* first-choice votes.

An example from electionscience.org explores this scenario. In a hypothetical instant runoff election, called Election 1, candidate

A wins. Although A and B have the same number of first-choice votes, neither has the majority required to win (nine out of 17 votes). So C, having the fewest first-choice votes is removed from contention, and the ballots are adjusted to fill C's gaps, yielding a majority for candidate A.

Now imagine a separate scenario called Election 2, where everybody votes in the same way as in Election 1 except for two people who upgrade A from their third choice to their first choice. Amazingly, even though A won Election 1 and now has more first-choice votes than before, C becomes the new victor. This is because upgrading A results in downgrading B so that B is now the candidate with the fewest first-choice votes. When B is removed, A doesn't fare as well in a head-to-head against C as they did against B in Election 1.

This counterintuitive phenomenon occurred in Burlington, Vt.'s 2009 mayoral election where Progressive Party member Bob Kiss beat the Republican and Democratic nominees in an instant runoff election. Amazingly, if more voters had placed Kiss first in their ranking, he would have lost the election.

Condorcet methods, named after 18th-century French mathematician and political philosopher Marquis de Condorcet, elect a candidate who would win in a head-to-head election against any other candidate. For example, suppose that in an election without any third-party candidates Al Gore would have beaten George W. Bush in 2000. Gore certainly would have won head-to-head contests with any one of the third-party candidates as well. Gore winning any hypothetical one-on-one election would make him a so-called Condorcet candidate. It seems obvious that such a candidate should be the victor because the population prefers them to all of their opponents. But here's an important snag in electing Condorcet candidates: they don't always exist. Voter preferences can be cyclic such that the population prefers A to B and B to C but also prefers C to A. This violation of transitivity is known as the Condorcet paradox (and is reminiscent of intransitive dice, which I wrote about recently).

Several other schemes for amalgamating ranked votes into a winner have been proposed. They each have their pros and cons, and, even more unsettling, the outcome of an election can entirely depend on which system gets used.

The same simple election can yield different results under each of the three systems we've discussed. This comparison leads to a hopeful question: Is there a perfect ranked-choice voting system? Perhaps we just have yet to discover the ideal design that maximally represents the interest of the public while avoiding the pitfalls of existing proposals. Nobel Prize–winning economist Kenneth Arrow investigated this question and came up with bare minimum requirements of any reasonable aggregator, or method that converts voter rankings into one societal ranking:

1. Unanimity: If every person in the population ranks candidate A above candidate B, then the aggregator should put candidate A above candidate B.

2. Independence of irrelevant alternatives: Suppose the aggregator puts candidate A above B. If voters were to change some of their rankings *but everybody kept their relative order of A vs. B the same,* then A should remain above B in the new aggregate ranking. The societal ordering of A and B should depend only on individual orderings of A and B and not those of other candidates.

The commonsensical list sets a low bar. But Arrow proved a striking fact that has come to be known as Arrow's impossibility theorem: there is only one type of aggregator that satisfies both conditions, a dictatorship. By a dictatorship, Arrow means a ridiculous aggregator that simply always mimics the rankings of the same single voter. No ranked choice voting scheme, regardless of how clever or complex it is, can simultaneously satisfy unanimity and independence of irrelevant alternatives unless it's a dictatorship. The theorem suggests that no ranked choice voting scheme is perfect, and we will always have to contend with undesirable or counterintuitive outcomes.

This proof doesn't mean that we should scrap ranked choice voting. It still does a better job at capturing the will of the electorate than plurality voting. It simply means that we need to pick and choose which properties we want in our aggregator and acknowledge that we can't have it all. The theorem doesn't say that every single *election* will be flawed, but rather that no ranked-choice *electoral system* is invulnerable to flaws. Arrow has said of his own result: "Most systems are not going to work badly all of the time. All I proved is that all can work badly at times."

And the idealists among us should not lose hope, because ranked choice voting isn't the only game in town for souped-up electoral systems. Merely ranking candidates loses a lot of information about voter preferences. For example, here's a ranking of foods I'd like to eat from most desirable to least: vanilla ice cream > chocolate ice cream > my own sneakers. The ranking conveys no information about just how close my taste for vanilla and chocolate ice cream is nor my distaste for my Nikes. To properly express my desires, I should assign scores to the candidate meals to communicate not only which ones I prefer more but *by how much*. This is called cardinal voting, or range voting, and although it's no panacea and has its own shortcomings, it circumvents the limitations imposed by Arrow's impossibility theorem, which only applies to ranked choice voting.

We're all familiar with cardinal voting. In Olympic gymnastics, judges decide the winner by giving numeric scores to the competitors, and whoever has the most total points at the end wins. Whenever you sort products by consumers' star ratings online you're presented with the winners of a cardinal election. Ancient Spartans elected leaders by gathering in an assembly and shouting for each of the candidates in turn. Whoever received the loudest shouts won the election. While this sounds crude to modern ears, it was actually an early form of cardinal voting. People could vote for multiple candidates and "score" them by choosing what volume of voice to contribute to the roar of the crowd. This is impressive considering that cardinal voting, despite granting the people more input than any of the other systems we've discussed, has never been used in a modern election. Perhaps we shouldn't be surprised: the ancient Greeks did invent democracy after all.

About the Author

Jack Murtagh writes about math and puzzles, including a series on mathematical curiosities at Scientific American and a weekly puzzle column at Gizmodo. He holds a Ph.D. in theoretical computer science from Harvard University. Follow Murtagh on X (formerly Twitter) @JackPMurtagh.

Section 2: Public Opinion

Presidential Debates Have Shockingly Little Effect on Election Outcomes

By Rachel Nuwer

The first 2020 presidential debate did not go well for Donald Trump. Viewers were turned off by the president's constant hectoring of Joe Biden. And many were alarmed when he not only declined to denounce white supremacists but went so far as to tell a far-right neofascist group to "stand by." Polling by FiveThirtyEight revealed that 50 percent of people who watched the event rated Trump's performance as "very poor."

But while Biden clearly won the debate, this does not mean he will win the election. Studies indicate that televised presidential debates have very little, if any, impact on votes. For a variety of reasons, this observation is especially true in 2020.

"People aren't really watching debates because they're like, 'I'm gonna take this time and really compare these two candidates on their merits,'" says Yanna Krupnikov, a political scientist at Stony Brook University. Most people watching have already chosen their candidate, she says, and even if that candidate does not perform well, "they already have a decision as to how they're going to vote."

For years, researchers have suspected presidential debates have a tiny to nonexistent influence on election outcomes. Most studies have focused on a single debate or election, however, limiting their ability to weed out potential confounding variables. "Some people are heralding the debate [in late September] as the one that mattered," says Christopher Wlezien, a professor of government at the University of Texas at Austin. "But if you look at public opinion polls, it's hard to really partition these things out." The almost concurrent news that Trump and others in his administration contracted COVID-19 may have had a more consequential effect on people's views of the candidate.

To cut through such noise, in 2019 Vincent Pons, an associate professor at Harvard Business School, and graduate student Caroline Le Pennec of the University of California, Berkeley, produced a working paper analyzing the influence of 56 TV debates on 31 elections in the U.S., the U.K., Germany, Canada and three other countries. The researchers' data set included 94,000 respondents who were interviewed before and after an election to see who they planned to vote for and who they actually wound up choosing. The surveys took place in the two months leading up to an election, with a different set of individuals interviewed each day. This approach allowed the researchers to determine the percentage of people who had settled on their final choice as election day grew nearer and to test for any effect immediately before and after a debate.

Across all voting systems and election types, Pons and Le Pennec found that debates neither helped undecided voters to make up their mind nor caused those who had already made a decision to switch candidates. "I was surprised," Pons says. "If you look at the numbers of people watching TV debates and at all the media attention around debates, you would think debates matter."

Pons's study is not the only one to conclude that debates do not, in fact, have an impact. Wlezien arrived at the same finding when he and Robert Erikson of Columbia University analyzed all available U.S. presidential election polls between 1952, when the first televised debate took place, and 2012. The best predictor for a candidate's standing after a debate season, they found, is what it was before that person's face-offs.

A variety of factors likely contribute to the ineffectiveness of presidential debates in helping individuals to decide how to vote. For starters, many of the people who take the time to watch debates are those heavily engaged in politics to begin with, Krupnikov says, so they have already committed to a particular candidate. In the U.S. especially, when an election actually takes place, candidates have been campaigning for months—giving Americans plenty of time to have already made up their mind. And even if something sensational does happen in a debate and causes a wider stir, the effects tend to be small and fade by the time of the election. "Debates are short-term events, so they have less effect on people's choices," Wlezien says. "These performances just get added into this giant pile of information."

Also, unlike many other developed countries, the U.S. has only two major political parties—a dichotomy that contributes to deep ideological divides and a strong us-versus-them mentality. The two-party system likely lends weight to Pons's finding: compared with citizens of other countries, American voters are significantly less likely to change their decision in the two months leading up to an election.

Given all of these observations, most people who watch debates do not view them to be persuaded but to "see how their candidate is going to dominate, smear or embarrass the other candidate," says Jay Van Bavel, an associate professor of psychology and neural science at New York University. Regardless of what actually transpires in a debate, evidence also indicates that many viewers filter what they see in a way that aligns with their goals and identity. In unpublished results from a new study, Van Bavel found that, depending on which political party they belong to, people shown clips from a 2016 debate between Hillary Clinton and Trump selectively paid attention to different parts and remembered what happened differently. "When partisans tune into a debate, they often walk away with an opinion that just confirms what they believed before the debate began," Van Bavel says.

Presidential debates for the current U.S. election are probably even more subject to these forces than usual. Political polarization is at an extreme high, and voters are already well acquainted with both candidates from their years in office. "The more knowledge you have of someone, the more crystalized your attitude about them is," Van Bavel says. Additionally, early voting is happening at record levels. Millions of people have already cast their ballot, making the final presidential debate especially inconsequential.

"There's something very counterintuitive about telling people that, actually, this debate probably won't matter at all," Van Bavel says. "The things that will matter in this election—probably more than any other—are voter turnout, voter registration and early voting."

About the Author

Rachel Nuwer is a freelance science journalist and author who regularly contributes to Scientific American, *the* New York Times *and* National Geographic, *among other publications. Follow Nuwer on X (formerly Twitter) @RachelNuwer.*

How the Best Forecasters Predict Events Such as Election Outcomes

By Pavel Atanasov

The classic interview question that every applicant dreads: tell me about a time when you changed your mind. Most interviewees launch into some canned story about a sudden revelation—an aha moment of transformative insight—intended to demonstrate the candidate's candor, open-mindedness and analytic skills. The interviewer nods along as they consider if the story is memorable and thoughtful enough to score the candidate that job offer.

But is suddenly changing your mind really a mark of insight? Major revelations make for memorable stories, but our research shows they rarely represent how the best analytic minds revise their beliefs. Rather than doing a 180, those who excel at making accurate predictions tend to change their beliefs gradually. They revise their predictions to reflect new information, but they do so slowly, comparing it with the information they had before.

Most of us do not spend our lives forecasting the future, but any decision we make depends, in part, on our implicit predictions. Who we vote for, what jobs we take and even whether we carry an umbrella out the door all reflect our best guesses about the future: what a political candidate will do if elected, what job is the best fit, the chance of rain that day.

To understand the science of accurate predictions, the Good Judgment Project, a research effort led by Barbara Mellers and Philip Tetlock, where I was a postdoctoral scholar, recruited thousands of volunteer forecasters and asked them nearly 500 questions about the future. Generally geopolitical, these questions focused on topics such as "Will Angela Merkel win the 2013 election for chancellor of Germany?" or "Will there be a significant outbreak of H5N1 in China in 2012?" The participants' answers were probabilistic. For example, a forecaster might predict that Merkel had an 80 percent

47

chance of winning reelection. Over the course of the four-year study, sponsored by the U.S. intelligence agency Intelligence Advanced Research Projects Activity (IARPA), the team collected more than one million predictive judgments.

Out of the thousands of participants, the Good Judgment Project identified so-called "superforecasters," those who demonstrated uncanny skills in predicting the future and even did so better than intelligence analysts with access to classified information. To become a superforecaster, volunteers had to make consistently accurate predictions across dozens of questions over a period of at least nine months. Accuracy was the gold standard for talent spotting, but watching the results play out took time. So we hunted for other early clues about who might be especially good at prediction. And one promising clue was the way that forecasters updated their beliefs.

For years, psychologists, political scientists and businesspeople alike have studied how individuals change their mind—and, more specifically, how they revise the probabilities in their head. An example of this revision is when we see a dark sky from the window at noon and project that the chances of rain have gone up from 40 to 80 percent. Changing one's assessment can be a sign of open-mindedness. As Amazon founder Jeff Bezos has noted, people who are right a lot also change their mind a lot.

But big changes—for example, jumping from 40 to 80 percent—are not necessarily a sign that someone is open-minded. Such sudden reversals may instead be triggered by recency bias, the tendency to overemphasize new information. Sudden changes may also be caused by the availability heuristic, which makes us overemphasize facts and stories that come to mind easily, although not necessarily those that help us predict what's ahead. Good forecasters resist these tendencies and avoid overreacting to new or particularly memorable information.

The best forecasters must learn to navigate the twin risks of underreaction and overreaction. To find these individuals, we measured their belief-updating tendencies based on three criteria: frequency, confirmation and magnitude. Frequency is how often a person changes their beliefs about a question. Confirmation propensity is the habit of confirming one's previous beliefs and sticking to the original answer. And magnitude is how much each revision has changed on the probability scale.

We found that individuals with high confirmation propensity were generally inaccurate forecasters—they tended to assign high probability to events that did not happen and low probability to events that did occur. In contrast, those who updated their beliefs frequently were highly accurate forecasters. Finally, individuals who updated their beliefs in small increments outperformed their peers who made more drastic changes.

Like Aesop's proverbial tortoise, frequent updaters showed better subject-matter knowledge, more open-mindedness and a higher work rate. They were not always spot on with their initial forecasts, but their willingness to change their opinion allowed them to excel over time.

In contrast, incremental updaters resembled Aesop's hare: they were not especially hardworking, knowledgeable or open-minded. But they scored well on tests of fluid intelligence—which included questions on logical, spatial and mathematical reasoning—and were unusually accurate with their initial estimates for a question.

The best forecasters combined the good qualities of both the tortoise and the hare. The pattern of frequent incremental forecast revisions was a reliable mark of being good at prediction.

How forecasters update their beliefs is a very personal process, drawing on different thinking styles, life philosophies and predictive abilities. But despite this fact, belief-updating techniques can also be taught. We know, because we tested them. We randomly assigned approximately half of the subjects to receive a one-hour predictive-training intervention, while the other half, the control group, received no training. Interestingly, the forecasters who received training subsequently updated their beliefs in more frequent, smaller steps and achieved better accuracy than the control group.

The training materials did not explicitly tell forecasters to make smaller updates. Rather we provided general lessons that they could apply to their practice to balance their initial intuitions.

First, when we encounter opposing evidence, we often ignore one piece in favor of the other. For example, if we come across two election polls, one showing our favored candidate in the lead and the other showing that person trailing, most individuals choose the preferred poll and discount the other as inaccurate. As a forecaster, however, the best tactic would be to average the two. Averaging is generally less work, but it also requires us to compromise and entertain an idea that contradicts our beliefs.

Second, training also helped participants overcome what psychologists Amos Tversky and Daniel Kahneman called the inside view bias, or the tendency to focus on the unique aspects of each situation. Rather than comparing a situation with other similar ones, we focus instead on what makes it unique. And as a result, we often give outsized weight to insignificant factors. For example, when predicting the outcome of an election, we might concentrate on something such as yard signs as an indicator, although the signs are unique to our particular town and situation.

Conversely, the outside view is the practice of examining historical data and considering a given case as one of many. We may ask, "How often does the U.S. presidential candidate leading in mid-October go on to win in November?" To answer this question, we may then construct a reference class of, say, the past 10 presidential elections and count how many times the October poll leader won the general election. The resulting percentage—the base rate—is the outside-view answer. We can't all be master forecasters, but by taking the outside view and averaging conflicting data, we can inch closer to making better predictions.

About the Author

Pavel Atanasov is a decision psychologist who studies prediction. He is co-founder of the company Pytho and a co-principal investigator of the Human Forest project, both with Regina Joseph. Prior to that, he was postdoctoral scholar at the Good Judgment Project. Follow him on X (formerly Twitter) at @paveldatanasov.

Why Polls Were Mostly Wrong

By Gloria Dickie

In the weeks leading up to the November 2016 election, polls across the country predicted an easy sweep for Democratic nominee Hillary Clinton. From Vanuatu to Timbuktu, everyone knows what happened. Media outlets and pollsters took the heat for failing to project a victory for Donald Trump. The polls were ultimately right about the popular vote. But they missed the mark in key swing states that tilted the Electoral College toward Trump.

This time, prognosticators made assurances that such mistakes were *so* 2016. But as votes were tabulated on November 3, nervous viewers and pollsters began to experience a sense of déjà vu. Once again, more ballots were ticking toward President Trump than the polls had projected. Though the voter surveys ultimately pointed in the wrong direction for only two states—North Carolina and Florida, both of which had signaled a win for Joe Biden—they incorrectly gauged just how much of the overall vote would go to Trump in both red and blue states. In states where polls had favored Biden, the vote margin went to Trump by a median of 2.6 additional percentage points. And in Republican states, Trump did even better than the polls had indicated—by a whopping 6.4 points.

Four years ago, Sam Wang, a neuroscience professor at Princeton University and co-founder of the blog Princeton Election Consortium, which analyzes election polling, called the race for Clinton. He was so confident that he made a bet to eat an insect if Trump won more than 240 electoral votes—and ended up downing a cricket live on CNN. Wang is coy about any plans for arthropod consumption in 2020, but his predictions were again optimistic: he pegged Biden at 342 electoral votes and projected that the Democrats would have 53 Senate seats and a 4.6 percent gain in the House of Representatives.

Scientific American recently spoke with Wang about what may have gone wrong with the polls this time around—and what bugs remain to be sorted out.

[An edited transcript of the interview follows.]

Q: How did the polling errors for the 2020 election compare with those we saw in the 2016 contest?

A: Broadly, there was a polling error of about 2.5 percentage points across the board in close states and blue states for the presidential race. This was similar in size to the polling error in 2016, but it mattered less this time because the race wasn't as close.

    The main thing that has changed since 2016 is not the polling but the political situation. I would say that worrying about polling is, in some sense, worrying about the 2016 problem. And the 2020 problem is ensuring there is a full and fair count and ensuring a smooth transition.

Q: Still, there were significant errors. What may have driven some of those discrepancies?

A: The big polling errors in red states are the easiest to explain because there's a precedent: in states that are historically not very close for the presidency, the winning candidate usually overperforms. It's long been known turnout is lower in states that aren't competitive for the presidency because of our weird Electoral College mechanism. That effect—the winner's bonus—might be enhanced in very red states by the pandemic. If you're in a very red state, and you're a Democratic voter who knows your vote doesn't affect the outcome of the presidential race, you might be slightly less motivated to turn out during a pandemic.

    That's one kind of polling error that I don't think we need to be concerned about. But the error we probably should be concerned about is this 2.5-percentage-point error in close states. That error happened in swing states but also in Democratic-trending states. For people who watch politics closely, the expectation was that we had a couple of roads we could have gone down [on election night]. Some states count and report votes on election night, and other states take days to report. The polls beforehand pointed toward the possibility of North Carolina and Florida coming out for Biden. That would have effectively ended the presidential race right there. But the races were close enough that there was also the possibility that things would continue. In the end, that's what happened: we were watching more counting happen in Pennsylvania, Michigan, Wisconsin, Arizona and Nevada.

Q: How did polling on the presidential race compare with the errors we saw with Senate races this year?

A: The Senate errors were a bigger deal. There were seven Senate races where the polling showed the races within three points in either direction. Roughly speaking, that meant a range of outcomes for between 49 and 56 Democratic seats. A small polling miss had a pretty consequential outcome because every percentage point missed would lead to, on average, another Senate seat going one way or the other. Missing a few points in the presidential race was not a big deal this year, but missing by a few points in Senate races mattered.

Q: What would more accurate polling have meant for the Senate races?

A: The real reason polling matters is to help people determine where to put their energy. If we had a more accurate view of where the races were going to end up, it would have suggested political activists put more energy into the Georgia and North Carolina Senate races.

And it's a weird error that the Senate polls were off by more than the presidential polls. One possible explanation would be that voters were paying less attention to Senate races than presidential races and therefore were unaware of their own preference. Very few Americans lack awareness of whether they prefer Trump or Biden. But maybe more people would be unaware of their own mental processes for say, [Republican incumbent] Thom Tillis versus [Democratic challenger] Cal Cunningham [in North Carolina's Senate race]. Because American politics have been extremely polarized for the past 25 years, people tend to [end up] voting [a] straight ticket for their own party.

Q: Considering that most of the polls overestimated Biden's lead, is it possible pollsters were simply not adequately reaching Trump supporters by phone?

A: David Shor, a data analyst [who was formerly head of political data science at the company Civis Analytics], recently pointed out the possibility that people who respond to polls are not a representative sample. They're pretty weird in the sense that they're willing to pick up the phone and stay on the phone with a pollster. He gave evidence that people are more likely to pick up the phone if they're Democrats, more likely to pick up under the conditions of a pandemic and more likely to pick up the phone if they score high in the domain of social trust. It's fascinating. The idea is that poll respondents score higher on social trust than the general population, and because of that, they're not a representative sample of the population. That could be skewing the results.

This is also related to the idea that states with more QAnon followers experienced more inaccurate polling. The QAnon belief system is certainly correlated with lower social trust. And those might be people who are simply not going to pick up the phone. If you believe in a monstrous conspiracy of sex abuse involving one of the major political parties of the U.S., then you might be paranoid. One could not rule out the possibility that paranoid people would also be disinclined to answer opinion polls.

Q: In Florida's Miami-Dade County, we saw a surprising surge of Hispanic voters turning out for Trump. How might the polls have failed to take into account members of that demographic backing Trump?

A: Pollsters know Hispanic voters to be a difficult-to-reach demographic. In addition, Hispanics are also not a monolithic population. If you look at some of the exit polling, it looks like

Hispanics were more favorable to Trump than they were to Clinton four years ago. It's certainly possible Hispanic support was missed by pollsters this time around.

Q: Given that the presidential polls have been off for the past two elections, how much attention should people pay to polls?

A: I think polling is critically important because it is a way by which we can measure public sentiment more rigorously than any other method. Polling plays a critical role in our society. One thing we shouldn't do is convert polling data into probabilities. That obscures the fact that polls can be a few points off. And it's better to leave the reported data in units of opinion [as a percentage favoring a candidate] rather than try to convert it to a probability.

It's best not to force too much meaning out of a poll. If a race looks like it's within three or four points in either direction, we should simply say it's a close race and not force the data to say something they can't. I think pollsters will take this inaccuracy and try to do better. But at some level, we should stop expecting too much out of the polling data.

About the Author

Gloria Dickie is an environmental journalist based in British Columbia, Canada. Her work appears in National Geographic, Wired, *the* New York Times, *and elsewhere.*

The Secret Sauce in Opinion Polling Can Also Be a Source of Spoilage

By Xiao-Li Meng

O n November 6, 2020, I woke up to a flood (for a statistician) of tweets about my 2018 article "Statistical Paradises and Paradoxes in Big Data (I): Law of Large Populations, Big Data Paradox, and the 2016 US Presidential Election." A kind soul had offered it as an answer to the question: "What's wrong with polls?" which led to the article going viral.

As much as I was flattered by the attention, I was disappointed that no one had asked "Why would anyone expect polls to be right in the first place?" A poll typically samples a few hundreds or thousands of people, but it aims to learn about a population many times larger. For predicting a U.S. presidential election, conducting a poll of size n=5,000 to learn about the opinions of N=230 million (eligible) voters is the same as asking just about two people out of every 100,000 voters on average. Isn't it absurd to expect to learn anything reliably about so many from the opinions of so few?

Indeed when Anders Kiær, the founder of Statistics Norway, proposed the idea to replace a national census by "representative samples" during the 1895 World Congress of the International Statistics Institute (ISI), the reactions "were violent and Kiær's proposals were refused almost unanimously!" as noted by former ISI President Jean-Louis Bodin. It took nearly half a century for the idea to gain general acceptance.

The statistical theory for polling might be hard to digest for many, but the general idea of representative sampling is much more palatable. In a newspaper story about Gallop Poll going to Canada (*Ottawa Citizen*, Nov 27, 1941), Gregory Clark wrote:

> "When a cook wants to taste the soup to see how it is coming, he doesn't have to drink the whole boilerful. Nor does he take a spoonful off the top, then a bit from the middle, and some from

the bottom. He stirs the whole cauldron thoroughly. Then stirs it some more. And then he tastes it. That is how the Gallup Poll works."

The secret sauce for polling therefore is thorough stirring. Once a soup is stirred thoroughly, any part of it becomes *representative* of the entire soup. And that makes it possible to sample a spoonful or two to assess reliably the flavor and texture of the soup, regardless of the size of its container. Polling achieves this "thorough stirring" via random sampling, which creates, statistically speaking, a miniature that mimics the population.

But this secret sauce is also the source of spoilage. My 2018 article shows how to mathematically quantify the lack of thorough stirring, and demonstrates how a seemingly minor violation of thorough stirring can cause astonishingly large damage because of the "Law of Large Populations" (LLP). It also reveals that the polling error is the product of three indexes: data quality, data quantity and problem difficulty.

To understand these terms intuitively, let's continue to enjoy soup. The flavoring of a soup containing only salt would be much easier to discern than a Chinese soup with five spices. *Problem difficulty* measures the complexity of the soup, regardless of how we stir it or the spoon size. *Data quantity* captures the spoon size, relative to the size of the cooking container. This shift of emphasis from only the sample size n to the sample fraction n/N, which depends critically on the population size N, is the key to LLP.

The most critical index and also the hardest one to assess is *data quality*, a measure of the lack of thorough stirring. Imagine some spice clumps did not dissolve completely in the cooking, and if they have more chance of getting caught by the cook's spoon, then what the cook tastes is likely to be spicier than the soup actually is. For polling, if people who prefer candidate B over A are more (or less) likely to provide their opinions, than the polling will overpredict (or underpredict) the vote shares for B than for A. This tendency can be measured by the so-called Pearson correlation—let's denote it by r—between preferring B and responding (honestly) to the poll.

The higher the value of $|r|$ (the magnitude of r), the larger the polling error. A positive r indicates overestimation, and a negative r underestimation.

The whole idea of stirring thoroughly or random sampling is to ensure r is negligible, or technically to ensure it is on the order of the reciprocal of the square root of N. Statistically, this is as small as it can be since we have to allow some sampling randomness. For example, for N=230 million, $|r|$ should be less than one out of 15,000. However, for the 2016 election polling, r was –0.005, or about one out of 200 in magnitude for predicting Trump's vote shares, as estimated in my article (based on polls carried out by YouGov). Whereas a half a percent correlation seems tiny, its impact is magnified greatly when multiplied by the square-root of N.

As an illustration of this impact, my article calculated how much statistical accuracy was reduced by $|r|$=0.005. Opinions from 2.3 million responses (about 1 percent of the eligible voting population in 2016) with $|r|$=0.005 have the same expected polling error as that resulting from 400 responses in a genuinely random sample. This is a 99.98 percent reduction of the actual sample sizes, an astonishing loss by any standard. A quality poll of size 400 still can deliver reliable predictions, but no (qualified) campaign manager would stop campaigning because a poll of size 400 predicts winning. But they may (and indeed some did) stop when the winning prediction is from 2.3 million responses, which amount to 2,300 polls that each have 1,000 responses.

What was generally overlooked in 2016, and unfortunately again in 2020, is the devastating impact of LLP. Statistical sampling errors tend to balance out when we increase the sample size, but systematic selection bias only solidifies when sample size increases. Worse, the selection bias is magnified by the population size: the larger the population, the larger the magnification. That is the essence of LLP.

When a bit of soup finds itself on a cook's spoon, it cannot tell itself that "Well, I'm a bit too salty, so let me jump out!" But in an opinion poll, there is nothing to stop someone from opting out because of the fear of the (perceived) consequences of revealing a particular answer. Until our society knows how to remove such fear, or the pollsters can routinely and reliably adjust for such selective responses, we can all be wiser citizens of the digital age by always taking polling results with a healthy dose of salt.

About the Author

Xiao-Li Meng is the Whipple V. N. Jones Professor of Statistics at Harvard University.

How Coin Flipping Can Make Polls More Accurate

By Dennis Shasha

A fter the noisy 2020 election season in the United States, journalists wrote extensively about the inaccuracy of preelection polls. They weren't the only ones. According to a report by the American Association for Public Opinion Research entitled *2020 Pre-Election Polling: An Evaluation of the 2020 General Election Polls*, 2020 polls were off by the largest magnitude in decades at both the federal and state levels. For example, a CNN poll predicted that Joe Biden would lead Donald Trump by 12 percentage points. Biden won by 4.5 points.

The writers of the report suggested some possible reasons why polls were so off that year. Among them:

1. Trump decried many polls as fake, likely discouraging his supporters from responding. Pollsters might not have overweighted a pro-Trump response enough compared to a pro-Biden response, giving Biden a higher apparent lead.

2. It might be that Democrats who responded to polls were more favorable to Biden than those who didn't. Similarly, Republicans who responded might have been less favorable to Trump.

The report noted that polls not only overestimated Biden's support; the polls also overestimated Democratic support in the Senate. This could point to a "shy Republican" phenomenon, which might have two causes. It could be that some Republicans didn't trust the polling institutions, as Nathaniel Rakich of FiveThirtyEight told me. This lack of trust could be partly rectified by having polling organizations come from across the political spectrum. But it also could be that the people participating didn't want to state their true preferences to a stranger, even about an overall Democratic/Republican choice.

With the 2022 election year underway, one way to counteract the "shyness" problem is for pollsters to give the people they survey plausible deniability. That is, a person should be able to respond to a question honestly, while preventing the pollster from knowing whether the answer is that person's actual opinion. This could be especially useful in countries having autocratic leaders who might wreak vengeance on dissenters.

The question is how to achieve deniability without sacrificing accuracy? Surprisingly, flipping a coin a couple of times might help. Here I'm borrowing ideas from Stanley Warner's work in 1965 and differential privacy. Such methods have been used for surveys.

Here's an example.

A fictitious country has an upcoming election in which the Tin Man is running against the Scarecrow. Shy voters do not want to admit to supporting the Scarecrow even though many secretly like him.

So the pollsters say to each participant: "Please don't respond right away. Instead move to a place where you're all alone and flip a coin. If it's heads, then come back and tell me your true preference. If it's tails, then please tell me Scarecrow regardless of your true preference." This was basically the scheme Warner came up with for surveys that might ask embarassing questions such as whether a respondent had for example evaded taxes, slept with a prostitute, etc.

Let's say, two hundred people answer the poll: 140 pick Scarecrow and 60 pick Tin Man. Given what the pollsters have told the pollees, roughly 100 people will respond "Scarecrow" regardless of their preference just because of the 50-50 probability of a coin toss; they flipped tails. Of the remaining 100 who flipped heads, 40 prefer Scarecrow and 60 prefer Tin Man, so Tin Man is the favorite.

What's the privacy advantage? If a person states a preference for Scarecrow, then that might have resulted just from a flip of the coin. Note also that the coin is just one way to introduce chance. Another might be to ask a participant to think of his or her best friend and to answer "Scarecrow" if that best friend's age were odd and honestly if even.

A few weeks later a scandal so much hurts Tin Man's reputation that, in some neighborhoods, it's dangerous for people to say they prefer Tin Man. So now the question is whether it's possible to conduct a new poll in such a way that any answer given by a participant enjoys plausible deniability.

Suppose the pollster gives the following instructions to people taking a new poll: "Please don't respond right away. Instead move to a place where you're all alone and flip a coin twice. If it comes up heads both times, then tell me 'Tin Man.' If it comes up tails both time, then tell me 'Scarecrow.' If you get one of each, please tell me your true preference."

There are 200 pollees. They sum up to 122 for Tin Man and 78 for Scarecrow. But of the 122 for Tin Man, 50 polled for Tin Man because of coin flips (two heads). Similarly, 50 polled for Scarecrow because of coin flips (two tails). So the actual polling result is 72 for Tin Man and 28 for Scarecrow. Tin Man is even more the favorite.

What has this puzzle taught us? For one thing, people in polls can enjoy plausible deniability on all sides of an issue (for the two candidates in our example). For another, the poll results will be accurate if the participants follow the rules, though more people may have to be polled to get the same statistical strengths. What remains to be seen is whether people who might take part in polls will even respond to a pollster and, if they do, respond honestly when the coin flips suggest they should. Primary season has begun; it's worth a try.

About the Author

Dennis Shasha is a professor of computer science at New York University.

Section 3: Political Psychology

Would You Vote for a Psychopath?

By Kevin Dutton

W as Adolf Hitler a psychopath? Would he meet the criteria established by modern psychiatry? These were the questions invariably raised by audiences in Germany when I would give talks there about my 2012 book *The Wisdom of Psychopaths*. Fortunately, I was in a position to answer them with data. In an ongoing study, I had been asking the official biographers of prominent historical figures to fill out, on their subject's behalf, an abbreviated version of the Psychopathic Personality Inventory–Revised (PPI-R). This short psychometric test uses 56 questions to quantify a person's psychopathic personality traits.

The Führer, predictably, scored very high. What *was* surprising—and of some consolation to my German audiences—was that so did British prime minister Winston Churchill. Although Hitler's scores suggested that he was a hole-in-one psychopath, the numbers I collected for Churchill—one of the most celebrated figures ever to grace the world political stage—put him, too, solidly on the green. What did that say about politicians in general? If one of the all-time greats scores high on the psychopathic spectrum, might not many lesser luminaries lie there as well?

Now seems like a particularly good time to consider this issue. The U.S. presidential race has brought a host of personalities to the fairway, so to speak. The so-called Goldwater rule, part of the American Psychiatric Association's ethical guidelines, deems it unethical for psychiatrists to comment on an individual's mental state without examining him or her in person. (Indeed, the rule came about because in the 1960s, a now defunct magazine called *Fact* polled clinicians about whether Senator Barry Goldwater was fit for the presidency.) But from the media this election cycle, there has been no shortage of armchair diagnoses declaring several of the front-runners to be narcissists, megalomaniacs or psychopaths.

Are any of the candidates who have thrown their hat into the race *really* psychopaths? The label is far from one-size-fits-all. Although for most people it brings to mind serial killers such as Ted Bundy and Jeffrey Dahmer, experts use the term specifically to refer to individuals with a distinct subset of personality characteristics, among them ruthlessness, fearlessness, self-confidence, superficial charm, charisma, dishonesty, and core deficits in empathy and conscience. And while no one likes a heartless liar, the fact is that none of these traits in and of themselves presents a serious challenge to mental health. Instead what distinguishes the cold-blooded murderer from a psychopathic president is a question of context and degree. As with any personality dimension, resting levels of psychopathic characteristics vary. Using measures such as the PPI-R, researchers can conduct fine-grained analyses of these different components to uncover potentially toxic or helpful combinations—mixes that assist or derail the people who possess them.

Several studies have now placed past U.S. presidents and historical leaders under this microscope, revealing intriguing patterns. My own research has found that there are particular psychopathic traits that can benefit leaders enormously and others that lead to disaster in office. Recently I turned my attention to men and women vying for the U.S. presidency, who were, at the time I was writing this article: Hillary Clinton, Ted Cruz, Bernie Sanders and Donald Trump. In a new study, I assessed their psychopathic traits in much the same way I analyzed Hitler and Churchill. My results, described below, may give U.S. voters something to think about come November.

Will the Real Psychopath Please Step Forward?

To understand psychopathy better, imagine a personality "mixing desk" on which its hallmark traits, as measured by the PPI-R, consist of a hodgepodge of knobs and sliders. It would feature eight dials grouped across three different regions of the console. Though disputed by some scholars, one area would be labeled Fearless Dominance and include three components: Social Influence, Fearlessness and Stress Immunity, which are all self-explanatory. Another section, called Self-Centered Impulsivity, would feature four traits: Machiavellian Self-

Interest, Rebellious Nonconformity, Blame Externalization and Carefree Nonplanfulness (a devil-may-care attitude toward the future). The third region would have a single dial: Coldheartedness.

If you could twiddle these controls in various combinations and see the results, you would soon arrive at two conclusions. First, there is no correct setting that defines all psychopaths. Depending on the timing and circumstances, individuals will constantly dial these traits up or down in search of the most effective alignment. And second, some jobs and professions—including management roles, business, law, the military, emergency services and surgery—demand that some of these dials are always cranked up a little higher than average. In general, high-risk, high-status positions place a premium on qualities such as decisiveness, mental toughness and emotional detachment—all of which are made easier by high settings on certain psychopathic qualities.

What specific mix serves as a psychological booster rocket in politics? To begin to find out, I conducted interviews with a number of British politicians and political commentators—from members of the House of Lords, to local elected officials, to well-known radio and TV anchors. They all deemed a few key traits to be indispensable for any politician. Foremost, they agreed that politicians must be able to make difficult decisions under considerable pressure. They need to be able to juggle many multifaceted crises, ranging from the threats posed by rogue nations to those caused by natural disasters. They have to be willing to send their country's young people to war in the certain knowledge that some will lose their lives. And they need excellent self-presentation skills and superficial charm—specifically, the ability to feign empathy even if they do not feel it. As Teddy Roosevelt once said: "The most successful politician is he who says what the people are thinking most often and in the loudest voice." (Indeed, some observers credit the rise of Donald Trump to precisely this, at least among a portion of the electorate.)

Finally, the politicians I interviewed noted that even to run for office, politicians need supreme self-confidence. It then takes that same kind of Teflon-coated self-belief and unrelenting focus to implement policy. Dealing with opponents often calls for considerable ruthlessness and mental toughness. As one senior British politician told me: "The only way to tell who's stabbing you in the back in politics is to see their reflection in the eyes of the person who's stabbing you from the front!"

The picture of an ideal candidate that emerged from this survey was one of a charming, persuasive, self-confident individual who can be ruthless when necessary and who is also heat-resistant: he or she can maintain focus, keep a cool head and perform under fire. In terms of our personality mixing desk, the best setting would be "high" on all the Fearless Dominance dials, variable for the Coldheartedness dial and low for the Self-Centered Impulsivity dials. Put another way, politics came out as a profession in which an official consignment of legalized, precision-engineered psychopathy would come in rather handy.

Our Fearless Leaders

Several years ago psychologist Scott O. Lilienfeld of Emory University, who co-developed the Psychopathic Personality Inventory and is a *Scientific American Mind* advisory board member, joined psychologists Steven Rubenzer, Thomas Faschingbauer and others in an intriguing collaboration. First, researchers handed out the latest iteration of the NEO Personality Inventory, which assesses the so-called big five personality traits, to biographers of, or experts on, every U.S. president up to and including George W. Bush. Just as in my study, these experts used their in-depth knowledge of their subjects to answer on the presidents' behalf. Based on these responses, Lilienfeld then extrapolated to what extent each president exhibited various psychopathic character traits. From these data, I subsequently created two top-10 lists, ranking the presidents' scores in Fearless Dominance and Self-Centered Impulsivity.

The results could not have been clearer. Similar to what I surmised from my survey of British politicians, higher settings on the Fearless Dominance dials were associated with higher ratings of presidential performance, leadership, persuasiveness, crisis management, perceived standing on the world stage and congressional relations. They were also linked to a number of more objective indicators of a president's performance, such as how many new projects he initiated. In contrast, higher settings on the Self-Centered Impulsivity dials were associated with indicators of an insalubrious interpersonal style—such as invoking congressional impeachment resolutions, tolerating unethical behavior in subordinates and having an unsavory reputation in general.

The findings also confirmed that biographers respond accurately enough to measures such as the PPI-R to reliably evaluate historical figures. For example, it is interesting to note that historians and political scientists consistently rate the two Roosevelts among the top-five greatest American presidents of all time, and in keeping with that assessment, they appear first and third on the Fearless Dominance top-10 list and are absent from the Self-Centered Impulsivity list. (Talk of Fearless Dominance: Teddy Roosevelt, after his 1912 electoral loss to Woodrow Wilson, set about exploring a previously uncharted tributary of the Amazon River, complete with piranhas, rapids and indigenous people bearing poison-tipped arrows!) In contrast, Andrew Johnson and Richard Nixon, who both feature on the Self-Centered Impulsivity top 10 but not on the Fearless Dominance list, are frequently cited among the worst.

My own ongoing study of historical figures is yielding similar profiles among the great, the good and the not so good. As with the full version of the PPI-R, the short version does not have a cutoff score at which nonpsychopaths end and psychopaths begin. Instead it represents scores as percentiles of normative response patterns found across the general population. So to put my results in context, it is useful to know the scores associated with the top 20 percent (or upper quintile) of the evaluated subjects for its various traits.

Among men, that means that if an individual scores in the upper quintile across the three broader dimensions (that is, 68 or above for Fearless Dominance, 69 or above for Self-Centered Impulsivity, and 18 or above for Coldheartedness), he would weigh in with a minimum total score of 155. For women, the same 80th percentile watermark falls a little lower at 62.4 for Fearless Dominance, 62 for Self-Centered Impulsivity and 15 for Coldheartedness, for a total of 139.4.

In my list of leaders, everyone from Emperor Nero and above—including Jesus and Saint Paul—has a notably high total score and a top quintile finish on at least one of the three dimensions. British prime minister Margaret Thatcher falls just short of this distinction. If, however, you consider the scores broken down by dimension, you do find that some esteemed leaders land below the top quintile. Both George Washington and Abraham Lincoln are high on Fearless Dominance but low in Self-Centered Impulsivity and so come out with relatively modest total scores. In short, they have all the "positive" aspects of a psychopathic personality—affording them mental toughness, social influence and boldness—with none of the negative characteristics, which manifest as impulsivity, egocentrism and insubordination. In contrast, Hitler had all the "bad" aspects of psychopathy and fewer of the "good" ones.

The 2016 Race

To evaluate the top candidates in the U.S. presidential race, I contacted one of the BBC's most respected and seasoned American political news anchors, whom I assured complete anonymity, and asked this individual to fill out the PPI-R short form on behalf of the four leading contenders at the time—Clinton, Cruz, Sanders and Trump. In each case, this anchor answered the questions by drawing on personal firsthand experiences with the candidates, as well as expert media analysis and dispassionate general impressions.

When the results were tallied, Trump trumped the rest of the field, achieving a total psychopathy score in league with Hitler and Idi Amin. Of particular note, he outscored the other three contenders in the Fearless Dominance dimension, associated with successful presidencies. At the same time, however, his "negative" psychopathic ratings were also higher than the other three candidates. Across all eight psychopathic traits, Cruz ran pretty much neck and neck with his Republican rival—but lost ground when it came to Carefree Nonplanfulness and Social Influence: in other words, his scores suggested he is less impulsive and less persuasive than Trump. In summary, the comparison between the two did not prove a knockout for Trump, but if it were a boxing match, he would have won a unanimous points decision with Cruz still on his feet at the final bell.

Among the Democratic contenders, Clinton and Sanders were fairly evenly matched on "positive" psychopathic traits—both scoring high on Social Influence and in the middle of the road on the rest. That said, the two diverged markedly on "negative" psychopathic characteristics, with Clinton's higher tally forming the basis of her significantly higher total score. At 152, Hillary surged a full 16 points higher than Thatcher, the U.K.'s only female prime minister. Allowing for the gender differences in percentile cutoffs, her score was more on par with Trump's.

"A leader takes people where they want to go. A great leader takes people where they don't necessarily want to go but ought to be," said Rosalynn Carter, wife of Jimmy Carter. The quote suggests that this first lady had some intuitive grasp of the idea that great political leadership entails cranking up *some* psychopathic dials on our personality mixing desk—those associated with fearlessness and dominance—while turning down the ones associated with self-centeredness and impulsivity. So far the research backs her up.

The Price of Greatness

What about leadership in nonpolitical spheres? In 2014 Lilienfeld and I, along with our colleagues, conducted a study that provided the first published data indicating a direct link between job status and psychopathic personality characteristics, drawing on an Internet-based survey of nearly 3,400 people. Specifically, we found that higher total scores on the short form of the PPI-R correlated positively, though modestly, with holding leadership and management positions. The association was significantly stronger for those attributes related to Fearless Dominance. We also found that people in high-risk occupations, such as police officers and firefighters, had much higher scores on all three PPI-R variables. Taken together, these studies support a particular view of what makes for an effective leader. Politicians and executives alike may not all be psychopaths (although some of them, of course, may well be). On the other hand, certain psychopathic traits—including mental toughness, social influence and fearlessness—do appear to be very useful in leadership roles and can help leaders to find considerable success.

These very same traits certainly helped Churchill. On July 3, 1940, early in World War II, he faced a standoff with the French at the port of Mers-el-Kébir in North Africa. In response to the Franco-German armistice of June 22, he dispatched a British task force to demand the surrender of the French battleships stationed there. The task force offered the French admiral three options to prevent the Germans from seizing his vessels: continue fighting the Germans; proceed under escort to a British port for repatriation after the war; or sail to a French safe haven in the West Indies. If he failed to comply, the British navy would scuttle the fleet.

The story does not end well. Churchill's brutal assault cost some 1,300 French sailors their lives. It was ruthless. It was fearless. And boy, was it decisive. It was also a political game changer. The indomitable resolve and unflinching fighting spirit demonstrated that day impressed Franklin D. Roosevelt and proved to be a major influence on the American decision to join forces with the Allies. The next U.S. president will also be poised to redirect world history. To make the right moves in a dangerous world, one can only hope that he or she possesses a similarly effective mix of psychopathic traits.

Referenced

Fearless Dominance and the U.S. Presidency: Implications of Psychopathic Personality Traits for Successful and Unsuccessful Political Leadership. Scott O. Lilienfeld et al. in *Journal of Personality and Social Psychology*, Vol. 103, No. 3, pages 489–505; September 2012.

Successful Psychopathy: A Scientific Status Report. Scott O. Lilienfeld et al. in *Current Directions in Psychological Science*, Vol. 24, No. 4, pages 298–303; August 2015.

About the Author

Kevin Dutton is a research psychologist at the University of Oxford and author of two popular science books, Flipnosis *and* The Wisdom of Psychopaths.

Donald Trump and the Psychology of Doom and Gloom

By Anne Marthe van der Bles and Sander van der Linden

I n the 2016 season finale of the late-night show "Last Week Tonight," host John Oliver called last year "the worst." The Oxford dictionaries declared "post-truth" word of the year and Donald Trump won the US presidential election with a campaign that stressed that American society is in decline. Opinion polls conducted in the final months of the campaign showed that 47% of Americans thought life for people like them in the country today is worse than it was 50 years ago; and 49% thought the future would be worse compared to life today. In the UK, the majority of the public voted for Brexit, in part, because of a general sense of discontent with the state of the country. Similarly, populist parties in Europe saw high levels of electoral support in response to messages that their countries are in dire straits.

Understandably, many people have tried to make sense of what happened. Take for example Trump's election in the United States: Commentators have argued that people voted for Trump because of economic anxiety, negative attitudes toward immigration, religion and race, and "a class rebellion against educated elitists." While many of these insights may contribute to an explanation, they do not reveal the whole story. For instance, the popular belief that Trump's voters were mainly working class turns out to be inaccurate.

Instead, new psychological research suggests that it is not necessarily citizens' personal (dis)content with their lives that matters as much as the perceived Zeitgeist of our time: a powerful shared feeling that society is taking a turn for the worse. In a recent study, one of us, along with colleagues at the University of Groningen, explored how the psychology of doom and gloom reveals how the spirit of our time is influencing people's decisions about divisive societal issues, such as voting for extremist parties.

Surprisingly, we found that a collectively shared sense of doom and gloom about society can exist among citizens who, individually, experience high personal well-being. Importantly, our study, conducted during the 2015 elections in the Netherlands, showed that it is this collectively shared sense of discontent about society that predicted whether people voted for extreme parties of the right and left, not people's discontent with their own lives.

This shared feeling of societal discontent can be conceptualized as an aspect of "Zeitgeist," the "spirit of the times." Looking back, it seems easy to identify the Zeitgeist of bygone times. For example, think about the Roaring 1920s, with economic prosperity, jazz music, and a general sense of novelty based on the introduction of many new technologies such as cars, movies, and radio. Or think about the Flower Power of the late 1960s, with anti-war movements, psychedelic music, and the Summer of Love. But how can we define and measure the Zeitgeist of our times?

Recent research has found a way to capture, at least in part, the "spirit of the time." We proposed that while Zeitgeist was originally a concept used by philosophers, it essentially describes a psychological experience. As such, in its broadest sense, the Zeitgeist can be defined as a collection of shared values, attitudes, norms, and ideas that exist within a society at a certain time. Measuring such a general phenomenon is difficult, but we found a way to capture the one aspect we were specifically interested in: our collectively shared awareness about the state of society, which currently is characterized by a sense of doom and gloom.

We reasoned that this sense of doom and gloom about society is rather tacit, applies to society as a whole instead of any one specific issue, and relates to something that intuitively "we all know to be true." Individuals have impressions about the extent to which people in general, are pessimistic or optimistic about the state of society. This implicit, generalized, collectively shared perception of how society is doing "colors" more specific ideas and judgments about society. When we think about, for example, what the state of unemployment is in the US or the extent to which the average

American encounters crime, one relevant source of information is this perception of society as a whole: If one's impression is that America as a whole is doing badly, then one would infer that the situation for a specific issue would be rather negative as well. If we flip this around, it means that if we ask people about their perceptions about a range of specific societal issues, we can extract their impression of the underlying state of society: a general factor Z.

We tested this method in three survey studies in the Netherlands and the US. To measure societal discontent as a general factor Z, we asked people to indicate on how many out of the last 30 days the average person had encountered problems with a range of 12 to 14 issues, such as crime, unemployment, and corruption. The results supported our idea: we could extract one dimension underlying people's perceptions about life in society, the general factor Z. In short, our approach assumes that there is a latent shared sense of societal (dis)content that influences how bad people perceive things to be for the average person across a range of issues and that this collective sentiment represents a key dimension of the reigning Zeitgeist.

In our recent study, we used this method to investigate whether societal discontent influenced voting for extreme parties. We conducted a field experiment during elections in the Netherlands in 2015. We asked people outside polling stations to fill in a short survey that included our Z-scale. The results showed that compared to the mainstream parties, people with more societal discontent were more likely to vote for the extreme right-wing party *PVV* (Party for Freedom) and the extreme left-wing party *SP* (the Socialist Party).

We also asked people how many problems they had encountered in their own lives using the same questions, to assess their personal level of discontent. We found that people thought that the average person experienced societal problems more than three times as often as they do themselves. It thus seems that people have a gloomy perception of what life is like for the average person. And, surprisingly, whereas societal discontent predicted voting for more extreme parties, people's personal discontent did not.

In our earlier research, we also investigated whether societal discontent influences how people interpret news headlines and media stories. We found that people with more societal discontent thought that negative news headlines, such as "US crime rates increase," were more likely to be true (while this one in particular is not true). They also were more likely to view society as being responsible for incidents that were portrayed in news stories, such as "body of man discovered after lying dead in his house for two years."

In short, if a sense of doom and gloom about society can influence people's voting behavior, it can influence the direction of a country—and it might already have for the US, the UK, and elsewhere. The idea that society is ill or broken and that someone should "shake things up" in order to change this can motivate people to vote for parties or individuals promising such change, even if people themselves do not directly feel the effects of a "broken" society. This seems to work for politicians promising change through a right-wing agenda, such as Donald Trump, as well as a left-wing agenda, such as Bernie Sanders. An important implication of this research is that societal discontent is not about one specific issue, but rather about a range of issues: People are worried about the economy, *and* immigration, *and* healthcare, *and* crime and safety.

So how does this sense of doom and gloom about society emerge and evolve over time? Although we can only speculate at this point, it is evident that our perceptions about reality are partly shaped by the media, who often invoke cynicism rather than optimism about society. In addition, polarization might be an important factor. For example, when polled about the state of the economy, 83% of Clinton voters thought things were "excellent" whereas 79% of Trump voters thought the economy was doing "poorly." It is therefore perfectly possible for people who are satisfied with their personal lives to be gloomy about society, and vice versa. In short, in understanding the psychology of doom and gloom, it is key to distinguish people's (dis)content about their personal lives from the knowledge and ideas we collectively share that determine the context of our time. As Philosopher George Hegel once wrote "no individual can surpass their own time, for the spirit of their time, is also their own spirit." Be that as it may, perhaps we can take solace in the fact that we have some power over how we each choose to see the world, and by extension, that offers prospects for the emergence of a more positive and maybe even an optimistic, Zeitgeist.

About the Authors

Anne Marthe van der Bles is a postdoctoral research associate in the Cambridge Social-Decision-Making Lab at the University of Cambridge and a postdoctoral by-fellow at Churchill College, Cambridge. She recently completed her PhD in Social Psychology at the University of Groningen.

Sander van der Linden is a professor of psychology at the University of Cambridge and author of Foolproof: Why Misinformation Infects our Minds and How to Build Immunity.

Are Toxic Political Conversations Changing How We Feel about Objective Truth?

By Matthew Fisher, Joshua Knobe, Brent Strickland and Frank C. Keil

I n a key moment of the final 2016 Trump-Clinton presidential debate, Donald Trump turned to a question regarding Russian president Vladimir Putin:

"He has no respect for her," Trump said, pointing at Hillary Clinton. "Putin, from everything I see, has no respect for this person."

The two debaters then drilled down to try and gain a more nuanced understanding of the difficult policy issues involved. Clinton said,

"Are you suggesting that the aggressive approach I propose would actually fail to deter Russian expansionism?"

To which Trump responded,

"No, I certainly agree that it would deter Russian expansionism; it's just that it would also serve to destabilize the ..."

Just kidding. That's not at all what happened. Actually each side aimed to attack and defeat the other. Clinton really said,

"Well, that's because he'd rather have a puppet as president of the United States."

To which Trump retorted,

"You're the puppet!"

Episodes like this one have become such a staple of contemporary political discourse that it is easy to forget how radically different they are from disputes we often have in ordinary life. Consider a couple of friends trying to decide on a restaurant for dinner. One might say, "Let's try the new Indian restaurant tonight. I haven't had Indian for months." To which another replies, "You know, I saw that place is getting poor reviews. Let's grab some pizza instead?" "Good to know—pizza it is," says the first. Each comes in with an opinion.

They begin a discussion in which each presents an argument, then listens to the other's argument, and then they both move toward an agreement. This kind of dialogue happens all the time. In our research, which involves cognitive psychology and experimental philosophy, we refer to it as "arguing to learn."

But as political polarization increases in the U.S., the kind of antagonistic exchange exemplified by the Trump-Clinton debate is occurring with increasing frequency—not just among policy makers but among us all. In interactions such as these, people may provide arguments for their views, but neither side is genuinely interested in learning from the other. Instead the real aim is to "score points," in other words, to defeat the other side in a competitive activity. Conversations on Twitter, Facebook and even YouTube comment sections have become powerful symbols of what the combativeness of political discourse looks like these days. We refer to this kind of discussion as "arguing to win."

The divergence of Americans' ideology is accompanied by an animosity for those across the aisle. Polls have shown that partisan liberals and conservatives associate with one another less frequently, have unfavorable views of the opposing party, and would even be unhappy if a family member married someone from the other side. At the same time, the rise of social media has revolutionized how information is consumed—news is often personalized to one's political preferences. Rival perspectives can be completely shut out from one's self-created media bubble. Making matters worse, outrage-inducing content is more likely to spread on these platforms, creating a breeding ground for clickbait headlines and fake news. This toxic online environment is very likely driving Americans further apart and fostering unproductive exchanges.

In this time of rising polarization, an important question has arisen about the psychological effects of arguing to win. What happens in our minds—and to our minds—when we find ourselves conversing in a way that simply aims to defeat an opponent? Our research has explored this question using experimental methods, and we have found that the distinction between different modes of argument has some surprisingly far-reaching effects. Not only does it change people's way of thinking about the debate and the people on the opposing side, but it also has a more fundamental effect on our way of understanding the very issue under discussion.

Are We Oobjectivists or Relativists?

The question of moral and political objectivity is notoriously thorny, one that philosophers have been debating for millennia. Still, the core of the question is easy enough to grasp by considering a few hypothetical conversations. Consider a debate about a perfectly straightforward question in science or mathematics. Suppose two friends are working together on a problem and find themselves disagreeing about the solution:

Mary: The cube root of 2,197 is 13.

Susan: No, the cube root of 2,197 is 14.

People observing this conflict might not know which answer is correct. Yet they might be entirely sure that there is a single objectively correct answer. This is not just a matter of opinion—there is a fact of the matter, and anyone who has an alternative view is simply mistaken.

Now consider a different kind of scenario. Suppose these two friends decide to take a break for lunch and find themselves disagreeing about what to put on their bagels:

Mary: Veggie cream cheese is really tasty.

Susan: No, veggie cream cheese is not tasty at all. It is completely disgusting.

In this example, observers might take up another attitude: Even if two people have opposite opinions, it could be that neither is incorrect. It seems that there is no objective truth of the matter.

With that in mind, think about what happens when people debate controversial questions about morally infused political topics. As our two friends are enjoying their lunch, suppose they wade into a heated political chat:

Mary: Abortion is morally wrong and should not be legal.

Susan: No, there is nothing wrong with abortion, and it should be perfectly legal.

The question we grapple with is how to understand this kind of debate. Is it like the math question, where there is an objectively right answer and anyone who says otherwise must be mistaken? Or is it more like a clash over a matter of taste, where there is no single right answer and people can have opposite opinions without either one being wrong?

In recent years work on this topic has expanded beyond the realm of philosophy and into psychology and cognitive science. Instead of relying on the intuitions of professional philosophers, researchers like us have begun gathering empirical evidence to understand how people actually think about these issues. Do people tend to think moral and political questions have objectively correct answers? Or do they have a more relativist view?

On the most basic level, the past decade or so of research has shown that the answer to this question is that it's complicated. Some people are more objectivist; others are more relativist. That might seem obvious, but later studies explored the differences between people with these types of thinking. When participants are asked whether they would be willing to share an apartment with a roommate who holds opposing views on moral or political questions, objectivists are more inclined to say no. When participants are asked to sit down in a room next to a person who has opposing views, objectivists actually sit farther away. As University of Pennsylvania psychologist Geoffrey P. Goodwin once put it, people who hold an objectivist view tend to respond in a more "closed" fashion.

Why might this be? One straightforward possibility is that if you think there is an objectively correct answer, you may be drawn to conclude that everyone who holds the opposite view is simply incorrect and therefore not worth listening to. Thus, people's view about objective moral truths could shape their approach to interacting with others. This is a plausible hypothesis and one worth investigating in further studies.

Yet we thought that there might be more to the story. In particular, we suspected there might be an effect in the opposite direction. Perhaps it's not just that having objectivist views shapes your interactions with other people; perhaps your interactions with other people can actually shape the degree to which you hold objectivist views.

Winning vs. Learning

To test this theory, we ran an experiment in which adults engaged in an online political conversation. Each participant logged on to a website and indicated their positions on a variety of controversial political topics, including abortion and gun rights. They were matched with another participant who held opposing views. The participants then engaged in an online conversation about a topic on which they disagreed.

Half of the participants were encouraged to argue to win. They were told that this would be a highly competitive exchange and that their goal should be to outperform the other person. The result was exactly the kind of communication one sees every day on social media. Here, for example, is a transcript from one of the actual conversations:

P1: I believe 100 percent in a woman's choice

P2: Abortion should be prohibited because it stops a beating heart

P1: Abortion is the law of the land, the land you live in

P2: The heart beats at 21 days its murder [sic]

The other half of participants were encouraged to argue to learn. They were told that this would be a very cooperative exchange and that they should try to learn as much as they could from their opponent. These conversations tended to have a quite different tone:

P3: I believe abortion is a right all women should possess. I do understand that some people choose to place certain determinants on when and why, but I think it should be for any reason before a certain time point in the pregnancy agreed upon by doctors, so as not to harm the mother.

P4: I believe that life begins at conception (sperm meeting egg), so abortion to me is the equivalent of murder.

P3: I can absolutely see that point. As a biologist, it is obvious from the first cell division that "life" is happening. But I do not think life is advanced enough to warrant abolishing abortion.

It is not all that surprising that these two sets of instructions led to such results. But would these exchanges in turn lead to different views about the very nature of the question being discussed? After the conversation was over, we asked participants whether they thought there was an objective truth about the topics they had just debated. Strikingly, these 15-minute exchanges actually shifted people's views. Individuals were more objectivist after arguing to win than they were after arguing to learn. In other words, the social context of the discussion—how people frame the purpose of controversial discourse—actually changed their opinions on the deeply philosophical question about whether there is an objective truth at all.

These results naturally lead to another question that goes beyond what can be addressed through a scientific study. Which of these two modes of argument would be better to adopt when it comes to controversial political topics? At first, the answer seems straightforward. Who could fail to see that there is something deeply important about cooperative dialogue and something fundamentally counterproductive about sheer competition?

Although this simple answer may be right most of the time, there may also be cases in which things are not quite so clear-cut. Suppose we are engaged in a debate with a group of climate science skeptics. We could try to sit down together, listen to the arguments of the skeptics and do our best to learn from everything they have to say. But some might think that this approach is exactly the wrong one. There might not be anything to be gained by remaining open to ideas that contradict scientific consensus. Indeed, agreeing to partake in a cooperative dialogue might be an instance of what journalists call "false balance"—legitimizing an extreme outlier position that should not be weighed equally. Some would say that the best approach in this kind of case is to argue to win.

Of course, our studies cannot directly determine which mode of argument is "best." And although plenty of evidence suggests that contemporary political discourse is becoming more combative and focused on winning, our findings do not elucidate *why* that change has occurred. Rather they provide an important new piece of information to consider: the mode of argument we engage in actually changes our understanding of the question itself.

The more we argue to win, the more we will feel that there is a single objectively correct answer and that all other answers are mistaken. Conversely, the more we argue to learn, the more we will feel that there is no single objective truth and different answers can be equally right.

So the next time you are deciding how to enter into an argument on Facebook about the controversial question of the day, remember that you are not just making a choice about how to interact with a person who holds the opposing view. You are also making a decision that will shape the way you—and others—think about whether the question itself has a correct answer.

About the Authors

Matthew Fisher is an assistant professor of psychology at Southern Methodist University.

Joshua Knobe is a professor at Yale University, appointed both in the program in cognitive science and in the department of philosophy.

Brent Strickland is a researcher in cognitive science at the Jean Nicod Institute in Paris.

Frank C. Keil is Charles C. and Dorathea S. Dilley Professor of Psychology and a professor of linguistics and cognitive science at Yale University.

Psychological Weapons
of Mass Persuasion

By Sander van der Linden

W hen I was a teenager, my parents often asked me to come along to the store to help carry groceries. One day, as I was waiting patiently at the check-out, my mother reached for her brand new customer loyalty card. Out of curiosity, I asked the cashier what information they record. He replied that it helps them keep track of what we're buying so that they can make tailored product recommendations. None of us knew about this. I wondered whether mining through millions of customer purchases could reveal hidden consumer preferences and it wasn't long before the implications dawned on me: are they mailing us targeted ads?

This was almost two decades ago. I suppose the question most of us are worried about today is not all that different: how effective are micro-targeted messages? Can psychological "big data" be leveraged to make you buy products? Or, even more concerning, can such techniques be weaponized to influence the course of history, such as the outcomes of elections? On one hand, we're faced with daily news from insiders attesting to the danger and effectiveness of micro-targeted messages based on unique "psychographic" profiles of millions of registered voters. On the other hand, academic writers, such as Brendan Nyhan, warn that the political power of targeted online ads and Russian bots are widely overblown.

In an attempt to take stock of what psychological science has to say about this, I think it is key to disentangle two prominent misunderstandings that cloud this debate.

First, we need to distinguish attempts to manipulate and influence public opinion, from actual voter persuasion. Repeatedly targeting people with misinformation that is designed to appeal to their political biases may well influence public attitudes, cause moral outrage, and drive partisans further apart, especially when we're given the false impression that everyone else in our social network is espousing the same opinion. But to what extent do these attempts to influence translate into concrete votes?

The truth is, we don't know exactly (yet). But let's evaluate what we do know. Classic prediction models that only contain socio-demographic data (e.g. a person's age), aren't very informative on their own in predicting behavior. However, piecing together various bits of demographic, behavioral, and psychological data from people, such as pages you've liked on Facebook, results from a personality quiz you may have taken, as well as your profile photo (which reveals information about your gender and ethnicity) can improve data quality. For example, in a prominent study with 58,000 volunteers, a Stanford researcher found that a model using Facebook likes (170 likes on average), predicted a whole range of factors, such as your gender, political affiliation, and sexual orientation with impressive accuracy.

In a follow-up study, researchers showed that such digital footprints can in fact be leveraged for mass persuasion. Across three studies with over 3.5 million people, they found that psychologically tailored advertising, i.e. matching the content of a persuasive message to an individuals' broad psychographic profile, resulted in 40% more clicks and in 50% more online purchases than mismatched or unpersonalized messages. This is not entirely new to psychologists: we have long known that tailored communications are more persuasive than a one-size-fits all approach. Yet, the effectiveness of large-scale digital persuasion can vary greatly and is sensitive to context. After all, online shopping is not the same thing as voting!

So do we know whether targeted fake news helped swing the election to Donald Trump?

Political commentators are skeptical and for good reason: compared to a new shampoo, changing people's minds on political issues is much harder and many academic studies on political persuasion show small effects. One of the first studies on fake news exposure combined a fake news database of 156 articles with a national survey of Americans, and estimated that the average adult was exposed to just one or a few fake news articles before

85

the election. Moreover, the researchers argue that exposure would only have changed vote shares in the order of hundredths of a percentage point. Yet, rather than digital footprints, the authors mostly relied on self-reported persuasion and recall of 15 selected fake news articles.

In contrast, other research combing national survey data with individual browser histories estimates that about 25% of American adults (65 million) visited a fake news site in the final weeks of the election. The authors report that most of the fake news consumption was Pro-Trump, however, and heavily concentrated among a small ideological subgroup.

Interestingly, a recent study presented 585 former Barack Obama voters with one of three popular fake news stories (e.g. that Hillary Clinton was in poor health and approved weapon sales to Jihadists). The authors found that, controlling for other factors, such as whether respondents liked or disliked Clinton and Trump, former Obama voters who believed one or more of the fake news articles were 3.9 times more likely to defect from the Democratic ticket in 2016, including abstention. Thus, rather than focusing on just voter persuasion, this correlational evidence hints at the possibility that fake news might also lead to voter suppression. This makes sense in that the purpose of fake news is often not to convince people of "alternative facts," but rather to sow doubt and to disengage people politically, which can undermine the democratic process, especially when society's future hinges on small differences in voting preferences.

In fact, the second common misunderstanding revolves around the impact of "small" effects: small effects can have big consequences. For example, in a 61-million-person experiment published in *Nature*, researchers show that political mobilization messages delivered to Facebook users directly impacted the voting behavior of millions of people. Importantly, the effect of social transmission was greater than the direct effect of the messages themselves. Notably, the voter persuasion rate in that study, was around 0.39%, which seems really small, but it actually translates into 282,000 extra votes cast. If you think about major elections, such as Brexit (51.9% vs. 48.1%) or the fact that Hillary ultimately lost the election by about 77,000 votes, contextually, such small effects suddenly matter a great deal.

In short, it is important to remember that psychological weapons of mass persuasion do not need to be based on highly accurate models, nor do they require huge effects across the population in order to have the ability to undermine the democratic process. In addition, we are only seeing a fraction of the data, which means that scientific research may well be underestimating the influence of these tools. For example, most academic studies use self-reported survey experiments, which do not always accurately simulate the true social dynamics in which online news consumption takes place. Even when Facebook downplayed the importance of the echo chamber effect in their own *Science* study, the data was based on a tiny snapshot of users (i.e. those who declared their political ideology or about 4% of the total Facebook population). Furthermore, predictive analytics companies do not go through ethical review boards or run highly controlled studies using one or two messages at a time. Instead, they spend millions on testing thirty to forty thousand messages a day across many different audiences, fine-tuning their algorithms, refining their messages, and so on.

Thus, given the lack of transparency, the privatized nature of these models, and commercial interests to over-claim or downplay their effectiveness, we must remain cautious in our conclusions. The rise of Big Data offers many potential benefits for society and my colleagues and I have tried to help establish ethical guidelines for the use of Big Data in behavioral science as well as help inoculate and empower people to resist mass psychological persuasion. But if anything is clear, it's the fact that we are constantly being micro-targeted based on our digital footprints, from book recommendations to song choices to what candidate you're going to vote for. For better or worse, we are now all unwitting participants in what is likely going to be the world's largest behavioral science experiment.

About the Author

Sander van der Linden is a professor of psychology at the University of Cambridge and author of Foolproof: Why Misinformation Infects our Minds and How to Build Immunity.

The Science of America's Dueling Political Narratives

By Laura Akers

W hatever else one might say about the Trump era in American politics, it's provided a wealth of data for scientists studying public opinion. For those of us interested in "metanarratives"—the stories that groups tell themselves about who they are and where they're headed—the 2016 and 2020 campaigns have been a gold mine.

Every vision of America has a metanarrative at its core. Are we a land of endless opportunity, a beacon for the world's huddled masses? Are we the world's lone superpower, throwing its weight around? Every institution, every social movement and every political campaign offers its own answers to questions like these, and for the people who believe these answers, these stories can be vital to their identity.

The science of metanarratives and how we respond to them is still in its infancy. Our research team, headed by psychologist Gerard Saucier, has uncovered the metanarratives typical of terrorists and genocidal leaders worldwide. More broadly, my own work seeks to understand how the structure and features of metanarratives can elicit emotional responses, and how social factors influence public reactions.

Emotions arise when we make comparisons relevant to our own needs and desires. We contrast our present circumstances with the future, the past and alternative versions of today. Improvements make us happy and inspire us; losses sadden or frustrate us. If we can blame someone else for our loss, we may become angry with them. And if we're faced with threats, our fear can motivate action. As with fiction, we can categorize metanarratives by their emotional "genres," such as progress (pride, optimism) or looming catastrophe (fear).

The metanarratives in U.S. presidential elections are usually predictable. Each party wants progress, although the Democratic and Republican "flavors" of progress tend to differ. Each party also wants the stability needed for progress to work, so that policies can have predictable outcomes. The party in office typically offers more progress, or preserving a Triumph its administration achieved; the other promises a course correction back toward its own goals.

Compared with the usual metanarratives, Donald Trump's 2016 campaign was much more dynamic. First, he introduced a restoration story line, a promise to "Make America Great Again." This story line contrasts an idealized past and potential future with a fallen present, creating more dramatic emotional contrasts than a course correction. But Trump didn't stop there. "Drain the Swamp" and even "Lock Her Up!" were examples of transformation—an abrupt end to "business as usual." His infrastructure expansion plans were classic Progress, and his nomination by the conservative GOP promised the stability valued by party faithful. Voters could latch onto whichever vision most resonated with them, ignoring the others. The drama in Trump's metanarratives excited new segments of the public and helps explain his appeal, both to Republicans and others (like 12 percent of previous Bernie Sanders voters). As cognitive scientists George Lakoff and Drew Westen remind us, it's emotion that wins elections.

If we like, we can picture Trump as an amateur scientist, conducting a rudimentary experiment to see if new metanarratives would inspire the public. Meanwhile, the Democrats tried an informal experiment of their own, weighing the motivational power of the usual progress/stability versus a Sanders "revolution" to sharply reorient government priorities. They concluded the temporary loss of stability from a transformation would cause too much collective anxiety, and went with Hillary Clinton, then Joe Biden.

Biden's early metanarrative choices had been vaguely along the expected course correction line, but by the Democratic National Convention he'd settled on a much stronger genre, the crossroads. Both his slogan, "Battle for the Soul of the Nation" and his references to "inflection points" portray America as at a critical juncture. In narrative terms, this story line sets up suspense between two possible outcomes—as Biden put it, "shadow and suspicion" versus "hope and light"—a suspense that makes our votes meaningful, as we each participate in its resolution.

Trump's reelection slogan, "Keep America Great," is a triumph storyline that logically follows a restoration, yielding pride and self-satisfaction, but anxiety if the achievement is vulnerable. His RNC speech also featured progress (such as "new frontiers of ambition and discovery"), a course correction (including "returning to full employment" and "rekindle new faith in our values"), and his own version of a crossroads: either "save the American Dream" or "allow a socialist agenda to demolish our cherished destiny."

Trump's kitchen-sink approach to conveying a vision for the country means we can't compare the effectiveness of one metanarrative against another. Such real-world experiments are impractical. However, we can still explore the factors influencing our reactions to different story lines.

The public doesn't accept every metanarrative it's offered. We tend to be loyal to the cultural beliefs favored by our social circles and encouraged by our leaders. Even then, some voters stay open to alternatives, if there's enough dissonance between the party line and their own experiences.

A useful analogy again comes from narrative science. Psychologist Keith Oatley has described three ways to read a book: deeply immersed, such that its emotional world becomes our own; reflectively exploring its ideas by making our own connections and thinking critically; or staying emotionally detached. Similarly, we can treat the metanarratives in our lives as truths we shouldn't question, potentially valid perspectives we can weigh and choose among, or just plain wrong. Trump favors a "full immersion" approach, with his affinity for sensory-rich rallies and his insistence on personal loyalty. Biden's give-and-take style aligns more with critical thinking. Which is not to say that there aren't reflective Republicans or unquestioning Democrats; of course there are.

My personal, untestable hypothesis is that the election's bottom line will be emotional. As they weigh the personalities, policies, and metanarrative visions offered by the candidates, voters may choose the one who best offers an end to 2020's turmoil. The newfound appeal of stability could be the deciding factor. And as formal science works to catch up with the intuitive "science" practiced by politicians, we may learn to better understand the functioning of metanarratives in action.

About the Author

Laura Akers, Ph.D. is a research psychologist at the Oregon Research Institute. Follow her work at http://meta-narrator.com or on X (formerly Twitter) @meta_narrator.

Conservative and Liberal Brains Might Have Some Real Differences

By Lydia Denworth

In 1968 a debate was held between conservative thinker William F. Buckley, Jr., and liberal writer Gore Vidal. It was hoped that these two members of opposing intellectual elites would show Americans living through tumultuous times that political disagreements could be civilized. That idea did not last for long. Instead Buckley and Vidal descended rapidly into name-calling. Afterward, they sued each other for defamation.

The story of the 1968 debate opens a well-regarded 2013 book called *Predisposed*, which introduced the general public to the field of political neuroscience. The authors, a trio of political scientists at the University of Nebraska-Lincoln and Rice University, argued that if the differences between liberals and conservatives seem profound and even unbridgeable, it is because they are rooted in personality characteristics and biological predispositions.

On the whole, the research shows, conservatives desire security, predictability and authority more than liberals do, and liberals are more comfortable with novelty, nuance and complexity. If you had put Buckley and Vidal in a magnetic resonance imaging machine and presented them with identical images, you would likely have seen differences in their brains, especially in the areas that process social and emotional information. The volume of gray matter, or neural cell bodies, making up the anterior cingulate cortex, an area that helps detect errors and resolve conflicts, tends to be larger in liberals. And the amygdala, which is important for regulating emotions and evaluating threats, is larger in conservatives.

While these findings are remarkably consistent, they are probabilities, not certainties—meaning there is plenty of individual variability. The political landscape includes lefties who own guns, right-wingers who drive Priuses and everything in between. There is also an unresolved chicken-and-egg problem: Do brains start out processing the world differently or do they become increasingly different as our politics evolve? Furthermore, it is still not entirely clear how useful it is to know that a Republican's brain lights up over X while a Democrat's responds to Y.

So what can the study of neural activity suggest about political behavior? The still emerging field of political neuroscience has begun to move beyond describing basic structural and functional brain differences between people of different ideological persuasions—gauging who has the biggest amygdala—to more nuanced investigations of how certain cognitive processes underlie our political thinking and decision-making. Partisanship does not just affect our vote; it influences our memory, reasoning and even our perception of truth. Knowing this will not magically bring us all together, but researchers hope that continuing to understand the way partisanship influences our brain might at least allow us to counter its worst effects: the divisiveness that can tear apart the shared values required to retain a sense of national unity.

Social scientists who observe behaviors in the political sphere can gain substantial insight into the hazards of errant partisanship. Political neuroscience, however, attempts to deepen these observations by supplying evidence that a belief or bias manifests as a measure of brain volume or activity—demonstrating that an attitude, conviction or misconception is, in fact, genuine. "Brain structure and function provide more objective measures than many types of survey responses," says political neuroscientist Hannah Nam of Stony Brook University. "Participants may be induced to be more honest when they think that scientists have a 'window' into their brains." That is not to say that political neuroscience can be used as a tool to "read minds," but it can pick up discrepancies between stated positions and underlying cognitive processes.

Brain scans are also unlikely to be used as a biomarker for specific political results because the relationships between the brain and politics is not one-to-one. Yet "neurobiological features could be used as a predictor of political outcomes—just not in a deterministic way," Nam says.

To study how we process political information in a 2017 paper, political psychologist Ingrid Haas of the University of Nebraska-Lincoln and her colleagues created hypothetical candidates from both major parties and assigned each candidate a set of policy statements on issues such as school prayer, Medicare and defense spending. Most statements were what you would expect: Republicans, for instance, usually favor increasing defense spending, and Democrats generally support expanding Medicare. But some statements were surprising, such as a conservative expressing a pro-choice position or a liberal arguing for invading Iran.

Haas put 58 people with diverse political views in a brain scanner. On each trial, participants were asked whether it was good or bad that a candidate held a position on a particular issue and not whether they personally agreed or disagreed with it. Framing the task that way allowed the researchers to look at neural processing as a function of whether the information was expected or unexpected—what they termed congruent or incongruent. They also considered participants' own party identification and whether there was a relationship between ideological differences and how the subjects did the task.

Liberals proved more attentive to incongruent information, especially for Democratic candidates. When they encountered such a position, it took them longer to make a decision about whether it was good or bad. They were likely to show activation for incongruent information in two brain regions: the insula and anterior cingulate cortex, which "are involved in helping people form and think about their attitudes," Haas says. How do out-of-the-ordinary positions affect later voting? Haas suspects that engaging more with such information might make voters more likely to punish candidates for it later. But she acknowledges that they may instead exercise a particular form of bias called "motivated reasoning" to downplay the incongruity.

Motivated reasoning, in which people work hard to justify their opinions or decisions, even in the face of conflicting evidence, has been a popular topic in political neuroscience because there is a lot of it going around. While partisanship plays a role, motivated reasoning goes deeper than that. Just as most of us like to think we are good-hearted human beings, people generally prefer to believe that the society they live in is desirable, fair and legitimate. "Even if society isn't perfect, and there are things to be criticized about it, there is a preference to think that you live in a good society," Nam says. When that preference is particularly strong, she adds, "that can lead to things like simply rationalizing or accepting long-standing inequalities or injustices." Psychologists call the cognitive process that lets us do so "system justification."

Nam and her colleagues set out to understand which brain areas govern the affective processes that underlie system justification. They found that the volume of gray matter in the amygdala is linked to the tendency to perceive the social system as legitimate and desirable. Their interpretation is that "this preference to system justify is related to these basic neurobiological predispositions to be alert to potential threats in your environment," Nam says.

After the original study, Nam's team followed a subset of the participants for three years and found that their brain structure predicted the likelihood of whether they participated in political protests during that time. "Larger amygdala volume is associated with a lower likelihood of participating in political protests," Nam says. "That makes sense in so far as political protest is a behavior that says, 'We've got to change the system.'"

Understanding the influence of partisanship on identity, even down to the level of neurons, "helps to explain why people place party loyalty over policy, and even over truth," argued psychologists Jay Van Bavel and Andrea Pereira, both then at New York University, in *Trends in Cognitive Sciences* in 2018. In short, we derive our identities from both our individual characteristics, such as being a parent, and our group memberships, such as being a New Yorker or an American. These affiliations serve multiple social goals: they feed our need to belong and desire for closure and predictability, and they endorse our moral values. And our brain represents them much as it does other forms of social identity.

Among other things, partisan identity clouds memory. In a 2013 study, liberals were more likely to misremember George W. Bush remaining on vacation in the aftermath of Hurricane Katrina, and conservatives were more likely to falsely recall seeing Barack Obama shaking hands with the president of Iran. Partisan identity also shapes our perceptions. When they were shown a video of a political protest in a 2012 study, liberals and conservatives were more or less likely to favor calling police depending on their interpretation of the protest's goal. If the objective was liberal (opposing the military barring openly gay people from service), the conservatives were more likely to want the cops. The opposite was true when participants thought it was a conservative protest (opposing an abortion clinic). The more strongly we identify with a party, the more likely we are to double down on our support for it. That tendency is exacerbated by rampant political misinformation and, too often, identity wins out over accuracy.

If we understand what is at work cognitively, we might be able to intervene and try to ease some of the negative effects of partisanship. The tension between accuracy and identity probably involves a brain region called the orbitofrontal cortex, which computes the value of goals and beliefs and is strongly connected to memory, executive function and attention. If identity helps determine the value of different beliefs, it can also distort them, Van Bavel says. Appreciating that political affiliation fulfills an evolutionary need to belong suggests we should create alternative means of belonging— depoliticizing the novel coronavirus by calling on us to come together as Americans, for instance. And incentivizing the need to be accurate could increase the importance accorded that goal: paying money for accurate responses or holding people accountable for incorrect ones have been shown to be effective.

It will be nearly impossible to lessen the partisan influences before the November 3 election because the volume of political information will only increase, reminding us of our political identities daily. But here is some good news: a large 2020 study at Harvard University found that participants consistently overestimated the level of out-group negativity toward their in-group. In other words, the other side may not dislike us quite so much as we think. Inaccurate information heightened the negative bias, and (more good news) correcting inaccurate information significantly reduced it.

"The biology and neuroscience of politics might be useful in terms of what is effective at getting through to people," Van Bavel says. "Maybe the way to interact with someone who disagrees with me politically is not to try to persuade them on the deep issue, because I might never get there. It's more to try to understand where they're coming from and shatter their stereotypes."

About the Author

Lydia Denworth is an award-winning science journalist and contributing editor for Scientific American. *She is author of* Friendship *(W. W. Norton, 2020).*

Section 4: Threats to the Electoral Process

How Misinformation Spreads— and Why We Trust It

By Cailin O'Connor and James Owen Weatherall

In the mid-1800s a caterpillar the size of a human finger began spreading across the northeastern U.S. This appearance of the tomato hornworm was followed by terrifying reports of fatal poisonings and aggressive behavior toward people. In July 1869 newspapers across the region posted warnings about the insect, reporting that a girl in Red Creek, N.Y., had been "thrown into spasms, which ended in death" after a run-in with the creature. That fall the *Syracuse Standard* printed an account from one Dr. Fuller, who had collected a particularly enormous specimen. The physician warned that the caterpillar was "as poisonous as a rattlesnake" and said he knew of three deaths linked to its venom.

Although the hornworm is a voracious eater that can strip a tomato plant in a matter of days, it is, in fact, harmless to humans. Entomologists had known the insect to be innocuous for decades when Fuller published his dramatic account, and his claims were widely mocked by experts. So why did the rumors persist even though the truth was readily available? People are social learners. We develop most of our beliefs from the testimony of trusted others such as our teachers, parents and friends. This social transmission of knowledge is at the heart of culture and science. But as the tomato hornworm story shows us, our ability has a gaping vulnerability: sometimes the ideas we spread are wrong.

In recent years the ways in which the social transmission of knowledge can fail us have come into sharp focus. Misinformation shared on social media websites has fueled an epidemic of false belief, with widespread misconceptions concerning topics ranging from the COVID-19 pandemic to voter fraud, whether the Sandy Hook school shooting was staged and whether vaccines are safe. The same basic mechanisms that spread fear about the tomato hornworm have now intensified—and, in some cases, led to—a profound public mistrust of basic societal institutions. One consequence is the largest measles outbreak in a generation.

"Misinformation" may seem like a misnomer here. After all, many of today's most damaging false beliefs are initially driven by acts of propaganda and disinformation, which are deliberately deceptive and intended to cause harm. But part of what makes disinformation so effective in an age of social media is the fact that people who are exposed to it share it widely among friends and peers who trust them, with no intention of misleading anyone. Social media transforms disinformation into misinformation.

Many communication theorists and social scientists have tried to understand how false beliefs persist by modeling the spread of ideas as a contagion. Employing mathematical models involves simulating a simplified representation of human social interactions using a computer algorithm and then studying these simulations to learn something about the real world. In a contagion model, ideas are like viruses that go from mind to mind. You start with a network, which consists of nodes, representing individuals, and edges, which represent social connections. You seed an idea in one "mind" and see how it spreads under various assumptions about when transmission will occur.

Contagion models are extremely simple but have been used to explain surprising patterns of behavior, such as the epidemic of suicide that reportedly swept through Europe after publication of Goethe's *The Sorrows of Young Werther* in 1774 or when dozens of U.S. textile workers in 1962 reported suffering from nausea and numbness after being bitten by an imaginary insect. They can also explain how some false beliefs propagate on the Internet. Before the 2016 U.S. presidential election, an image of a young Donald Trump appeared on Facebook. It included a quote, attributed to a 1998 interview in *People* magazine, saying that if Trump ever ran for president, it would be as a Republican because the party is made up of "the dumbest group of voters." Although it is unclear

101

who "patient zero" was, we know that this meme passed rapidly from profile to profile.

The meme's veracity was quickly evaluated and debunked. The fact-checking website *Snopes* reported that the quote was fabricated as early as October 2015. But as with the tomato hornworm, these efforts to disseminate truth did not change how the rumors spread. One copy of the meme alone was shared more than half a million times. As new individuals shared it over the next several years, their false beliefs infected friends who observed the meme, and they, in turn, passed the false belief on to new areas of the network.

This is why many widely shared memes seem to be immune to fact-checking and debunking. Each person who shared the Trump meme simply trusted the friend who had shared it rather than checking for themselves. Putting the facts out there does not help if no one bothers to look them up. It might seem like the problem here is laziness or gullibility—and thus that the solution is merely more education or better critical thinking skills. But that is not entirely right. Sometimes false beliefs persist and spread even in communities where everyone works very hard to learn the truth by gathering and sharing evidence. In these cases, the problem is not unthinking trust. It goes far deeper than that.

Trust the Evidence

Before it was shut down in November 2020, the "Stop Mandatory Vaccination" Facebook group had hundreds of thousands of followers. Its moderators regularly posted material that was framed to serve as evidence for the community that vaccines are harmful or ineffective, including news stories, scientific papers and interviews with prominent vaccine skeptics. On other Facebook group pages, thousands of concerned parents ask and answer questions about vaccine safety, often sharing scientific papers and legal advice supporting antivaccination efforts. Participants in these online communities care very much about whether vaccines are harmful and actively try to learn the truth. Yet they come to dangerously wrong conclusions. How does this happen?

The contagion model is inadequate for answering this question. Instead we need a model that can capture cases where people form beliefs on the basis of evidence that they gather and share. It must also capture why these individuals are motivated to seek the truth in the first place. When it comes to health topics, there might be serious costs to acting on false beliefs. If vaccines are safe and effective (which they are) and parents do not vaccinate, they put their kids and immunosuppressed people at unnecessary risk. If vaccines are not safe, as the participants in these Facebook groups have concluded, then the risks go the other way. This means that figuring out what is true, and acting accordingly, matters deeply.

To better understand this behavior in our research, we drew on what is called the network epistemology framework. It was first developed by economists more than 20 years ago to study the social spread of beliefs in a community. Models of this kind have two parts: a problem and a network of individuals (or "agents"). The problem involves picking one of two choices. These could be "vaccinate" and "don't vaccinate" your children. In the model, the agents have beliefs about which choice is better. Some believe vaccination is safe and effective, and others believe it causes autism. Agents' beliefs shape their behavior—those who think vaccination is safe choose to perform vaccinations. Their behavior, in turn, shapes their beliefs. When agents vaccinate and see that nothing bad happens, they become more convinced vaccination is indeed safe.

The second part of the model is a network that represents social connections. Agents can learn not only from their own experiences of vaccinating but also from the experiences of their neighbors. Thus, an individual's community is highly important in determining what beliefs they ultimately develop.

The network epistemology framework captures some essential features missing from contagion models: individuals intentionally gather data, share data and then experience consequences for bad beliefs. The findings teach us some important lessons about the social spread of knowledge. The first thing we learn is that working together is better than working alone because someone facing a problem like this is likely to prematurely settle on the worse theory. For instance, they might observe one child who turns out to have autism after vaccination and conclude that vaccines are not safe. In a community, there tends to be some diversity in what people believe. Some test one action; some test the other. This diversity means that usually enough evidence is gathered to form good beliefs.

But even this group benefit does not *guarantee* that agents learn the truth. Real scientific evidence is probabilistic, of course. For example, some nonsmokers get lung cancer, and some smokers do not get lung cancer. This means that some studies of smokers will find no connection to cancer. Relatedly, although there is no actual statistical link between vaccines and autism, some vaccinated children will be autistic. Thus, some parents observe their children developing symptoms of autism after receiving vaccinations. Strings of misleading evidence of this kind can be enough to steer an entire community wrong.

In the most basic version of this model, social influence means that communities end up at consensus. They decide either that vaccinating is safe or that it is dangerous. But this does not fit what we see in the real world. In actual communities, we see polarization—entrenched disagreement about whether to vaccinate. We argue that the basic model is missing two crucial ingredients: social trust and conformism.

Social trust matters to belief when individuals treat some sources of evidence as more reliable than others. This is what we see when anti-vaxxers trust evidence shared by others in their community more than evidence produced by the Centers for Disease Control and Prevention or other medical research groups. This mistrust can stem from all sorts of things, including previous negative experiences with doctors or concerns that health care or governmental institutions do not care about their best interests. In some cases, this distrust may be justified, given that there is a long history of medical researchers and clinicians ignoring legitimate issues from patients, particularly women.

Yet the net result is that anti-vaxxers do not learn from the very people who are collecting the best evidence on the subject. In versions of the model where individuals do not trust evidence from those who hold very different beliefs, we find communities become polarized, and those with poor beliefs fail to learn better ones.

Conformism, meanwhile, is a preference to act in the same way as others in one's community. The urge to conform is a profound part of the human psyche and one that can lead us to take actions we know to be harmful. When we add conformism to the model, what we see is the emergence of cliques of agents who hold false beliefs. The reason is that agents connected to the outside world do not pass along information that conflicts with their group's beliefs, meaning that many members of the group never learn the truth.

Conformity can help explain why vaccine skeptics tend to cluster in certain communities. Some private and charter schools in southern California have reported vaccination rates in the low double digits. And rates have been startlingly low among Somali immigrants in Minneapolis and Orthodox Jews in Brooklyn—two communities that have suffered from measles outbreaks.

Interventions for vaccine skepticism need to be sensitive to both social trust and conformity. Simply sharing new evidence with skeptics will probably not help because of trust issues. And convincing trusted community members to speak out for vaccination might be difficult because of conformism. The best approach is to find individuals who share enough in common with members of the relevant communities to establish trust. A rabbi, for instance, might be an effective vaccine ambassador in Brooklyn, whereas in southern California, you might need to get Gwyneth Paltrow involved.

Social trust and conformity can help explain why polarized beliefs can emerge in social networks. But at least in some cases, including the Somali community in Minnesota and Orthodox Jewish communities in New York, they are only part of the story. Both groups were the targets of sophisticated misinformation campaigns designed by anti-vaxxers.

Influence Operations

How we vote, what we buy and who we acclaim all depend on what we believe about the world. As a result, there are many wealthy, powerful groups and individuals who are interested in shaping public beliefs—including those about scientific matters of fact. There is a naive idea that when industry attempts to influence scientific belief, they do it by buying off corrupt scientists. Perhaps this happens sometimes. But a careful study of historical cases shows there are much more subtle—and arguably more effective—strategies that industry, nation states and other groups utilize. The first step in protecting ourselves from this kind of manipulation is to understand how these campaigns work.

A classic example comes from the tobacco industry, which developed new techniques in the 1950s to fight the growing consensus that smoking kills. During the 1950s and 1960s the Tobacco Institute published a bimonthly newsletter called "Tobacco and Health" that reported only scientific research suggesting tobacco was not harmful or research that emphasized uncertainty regarding the health effects of tobacco.

The pamphlets employ what we have called selective sharing. This approach involves taking real, independent scientific research and curating it by presenting only the evidence that favors a preferred position. Using variants on the models described earlier, we have argued that selective sharing can be shockingly effective at shaping what an audience of nonscientists comes to believe about scientific matters of fact. In other words, motivated actors can use seeds of truth to create an impression of uncertainty or even convince people of false claims.

Selective sharing has been a key part of the anti-vaxxer playbook. Before the 2018 measles outbreak in New York, an organization calling itself Parents Educating and Advocating for Children's Health (PEACH) produced and distributed a 40-page pamphlet entitled "The Vaccine Safety Handbook." The information shared—when accurate—was highly selective, focusing on a handful of scientific studies suggesting risks associated with vaccines, with minimal consideration of the many studies that find vaccines to be safe.

The PEACH handbook was especially effective because it combined selective sharing with rhetorical strategies. It built trust with Orthodox Jews by projecting membership in their community (although it was published pseudonymously, at least some authors were members) and emphasizing concerns likely to resonate with them. It cherry-picked facts about vaccines intended to repulse its particular audience; for instance, it noted that some vaccines contain gelatin derived from pigs. Wittingly or not, the pamphlet was designed in a way that exploited social trust and conformism—the very mechanisms crucial to the creation of human knowledge.

Worse, propagandists are constantly developing ever more sophisticated methods for manipulating public belief. Over the past several years we have seen purveyors of disinformation roll out new ways of creating the impression—especially through social media conduits such as Twitter bots, paid trolls, and the hacking or copying of friends' accounts—that certain false beliefs are widely held, including by your friends and others with whom you identify. Even the PEACH creators may have encountered this kind of synthetic discourse about vaccines. According to a 2018 article in the *American Journal of Public Health*, such disinformation was distributed by accounts linked to Russian influence operations seeking to amplify American discord and weaponize a public health issue. This strategy works to change minds not through rational arguments or evidence but simply by manipulating the social spread of knowledge and belief.

The sophistication of misinformation efforts (and the highly targeted disinformation campaigns that amplify them) raises a troubling problem for democracy. Returning to the measles example, children in many states can be exempted from mandatory vaccinations on the grounds of "personal belief." This became a flash point in California in 2015 following a measles outbreak traced to unvaccinated children visiting Disneyland. Then governor Jerry Brown signed a new law, SB277, removing the exemption.

Immediately vaccine skeptics filed paperwork to put a referendum on the next state ballot to overturn the law. Had they succeeded in getting 365,880 signatures (they made it to only 233,758), the question of whether parents should be able to opt out of mandatory vaccination on the grounds of personal belief would have gone to a direct vote—the results of which would have been susceptible to precisely the kinds of disinformation campaigns that have caused vaccination rates in many communities to plummet.

Luckily, the effort failed. But the fact that hundreds of thousands of Californians supported a direct vote about a question with serious bearing on public health, where the facts are clear but widely misconstrued by certain activist groups, should give serious pause. There is a reason that we care about having policies that best reflect available evidence and are responsive to reliabale new information. How do we protect public well-being when so many citizens are misled about matters of fact? Just as individuals acting on misinformation are unlikely to bring about the outcomes they desire, societies that adopt policies based on false belief are unlikely to get the results they want and expect.

The way to decide a question of scientific fact—are vaccines safe and effective?—is not to ask a community of nonexperts to vote on it, especially when they are subject to misinformation campaigns. What we need is a system that not only respects the processes and institutions of sound science as the best way we have of learning the truth about the world but also respects core democratic values that would preclude a single group, such as scientists, dictating policy.

We do not have a proposal for a system of government that can perfectly balance these competing concerns. But we think the key is to better separate two essentially different issues: What are the facts, and what should we do in light of them? Democratic ideals dictate that both require public oversight, transparency and accountability. But it is only the second—how we should make decisions given the facts—that should be up for a vote.

About the Authors

Cailin O'Connor is an associate professor of logic and philosophy of science. She is co-author of The Misinformation Age: How False Beliefs Spread *(Yale University Press, 2019). Both are members of the Institute for Mathematical Behavioral Sciences.*

James Owen Weatherall is a professor of logic and philosophy of science at the University of California, Irvine. He is co-author of The Misinformation Age: How False Beliefs Spread *(Yale University Press, 2019). Both are members of the Institute for Mathematical Behavioral Sciences.*

Smartphone Data Show Voters in Black Neighborhoods Wait Longer

By Daniel Garisto

O n November 8, 2016, tens of million of Americans went to vote at about 110,000 polling places. Most were in and out in under 10 minutes, but many still waited in line a long while—in some cases, for hours. Until now, a comprehensive nationwide account of how much time voters spent waiting was out of reach.

In a new study led by economist Keith Chen of the University of California, Los Angeles, researchers matched anonymous location data from 10 million smartphones to 93,000 polling places to create the most extensive map to date of voter wait times across the U.S. The results, reported in a preprint paper posted on arXiv.org on August 30, showed one very clear disparity: voters in predominantly black neighborhoods waited 29 percent longer, on average, than those in white neighborhoods. They were also about 74 percent more likely to wait for more than half an hour.

This study "was a totally, totally different way to try to measure this problem than what we've seen before—and it comes to the same conclusion," says Stephen Pettigrew of the University of Pennsylvania, an expert in voting wait time, who was not involved with the study.

Timing the Vote

Long lines at polling places have made headline after headline in recent years, and have been the subject of a flurry of research by political scientists. Many see protracted voting wait times not only as an inconvenience but as a civil rights issue.

"[It] really creates a barrier to the most vulnerable voters out there," says Sophia Lin Lakin, an attorney at the American Civil Liberties Union (ACLU). Minority voters often have less flexible work hours, she says, so lengthy wait times can reduce their ability to vote. Long lines are estimated to have deterred between 500,000 to 700,000 people from casting their ballot in 2012. These problems led to the creation of the Presidential Commission on Election Administration, which issued a 2014 report that set forth a standard: "No citizen should have to wait more than 30 minutes to vote."

Measuring how much time voters really spend waiting, though, is easier said than done. Previous studies have typically relied on two methods: self-reported surveys and in-person poll observers. Studies using these methods generally agreed on a basic result: in 2012 and 2016 the average nonwhite voter waited about twice as long as the average white voter. Poll observers can precisely track an individual's wait time, and surveys are generally quite accurate. But both methods suffer from limited reach; the most comprehensive prior study covered only 528 polling places.

This data gap is where the new method shines: Chen and his colleagues collected addresses for 93,658 polling places—80 percent of the U.S. total—and converted each into latitude and longitude coordinates, effectively creating a map of voting spots across the country.

Smartphones "ping," or send out data with their location, every few minutes on average. Using proprietary data from SafeGraph, a company that collects such information from smartphone apps, the researchers gathered pings that came from within 60 meters of a polling place during the 2016 presidential election. From this sample, they excluded people unlikely to be voters: for example, those who were in the area all day and thus likely to be poll workers, and those who were there for less than one minute and thus likely to be just passing by. After doing so, they ended up with a sample of more than 150,000 voters at around 40,000 polling locations. Using demographic data from the U.S. Census, Chen and his colleagues compared the wait times of voters by neighborhood—and found those in majority-black neighborhoods (as well as other non-white-majority neighborhoods) waited longer.

Although the wait times the researchers calculated are not as precise as past studies, which could identify individual voters,

Pettigrew says the results are a trustworthy indicator of this trend. By 2016 two thirds of all Americans owned a smartphone, and voters who did not have one would presumably have been just as likely to get stuck in line. The study contended that its method was, in fact, biased toward *not* finding a racial disparity in wait times: false positives—nonvoters who resembled voters, based on smartphone data—would have acted like random noise and should have made it hard to see an effect. But the difference between black and white neighborhoods remains clear.

Still, the smartphone method does not answer a key question: "What it doesn't tell us is why. What's going on here?" says Robert Stein, a political scientist at Rice University, who did not participate in the new research. "I would want to use it as a basis for doing further observational studies. You know, you just can't get that from the phone."

In the new study, the researchers acknowledged the phone data were only a proxy for voting wait time, which could result from anything—ballots that take a while to fill out, a lack of parking spaces or too few voting machines. "It basically tells us who's within 200 feet [60 meters] of a polling place on Election Day," says Charles Stewart, a political scientist at the Massachusetts Institute of Technology, who was also not involved in the research.

Suppressing Turnout

Unlike explicit methods of voter suppression, such as Jim Crow–era laws, long voting wait times do not necessarily result from a direct intent to discriminate. Previous studies have found that some areas—often those that are nonwhite—lack the resources to properly accommodate their voters.

But in a 2016 study, Stein and his colleagues did find one particular culprit for long lines: voter ID laws. In many states, voters who do not have a certain form of identification must fill out a provisional ballot, a time-consuming ordeal that can clog up a polling place. Like cars on a highway, even a single stopped voter can slow down the whole line. Areas with minority voters—who are less likely to have an ID—tend to be most affected by these laws, Stein says.

The past decade has seen numerous challenges to voting, including gerrymandering (manipulating districts in a way that politically disenfranchises some voters), voter-roll purges (challenging people's registration status to keep them from voting), and, in 2016, targeted disinformation campaigns to suppress black voters. "Significantly, the Supreme Court has neutered the core protection of the federal Voting Rights Act," says Wendy Weiser, director of the Democracy Program at the Brennan Center for Justice at New York University. Previously, states with a history of discriminatory voting laws had to receive clearance from the federal government before making any changes to voting practices. But since the court's 2013 decision, nearly 1,700 polling places—many in black and Latino neighborhoods—have been shuttered. In 2017 the ACLU of Georgia sued a county elections board in the state for closing several polling places without adequate notice (more than 200 voting precincts have been closed in Georgia since 2012). "From our perspective, that's an unconstitutional burden on these individuals' right to vote," Lakin says.

With the 2020 elections around the corner, the authors of the new study wrote that their method is an "easily available and repeatable tool to both diagnose and monitor" voting wait times. But getting these kinds of smartphone data is difficult because they are proprietary, and getting the locations of nearly 100,000 polling places is no mean feat. "It's an incredibly rich data set, and there would be huge opportunities for either [the study authors] or for other researchers to take what they have and build on it," Pettigrew says. "Putting the data out there would be a huge step in the right direction."

About the Author

Daniel Garisto is a freelance science journalist covering advances in physics and other natural sciences. He is based in New York.

Congressional Ignorance Leaves the U.S. Vulnerable to Cyberthreats

By Jackson Barnett

In the last U.S. presidential election, Russian hackers penetrated Illinois's voter-registration database, viewing voters' addresses and parts of their social security numbers. Election results were not affected, but the attack put intruders in the position to alter voter data, according to a report from the Senate Select Committee on Intelligence. The incursion was part of hacking attempts against all 50 states, and intruders will try even more vigorously in 2020, yet experts say Congress is doing little to improve defenses. The Brennan Center for Justice at New York University says states will need just more than $2.1 billion to upgrade election computer systems, yet last month the Senate approved only a fraction of that amount: $250 million.

One reason for the inadequate response is that elected representatives and their staffs are not tech savvy enough to understand the scope of the problems, says Lawrence Norden, director of the Election Reform Program at the Brennan Center and co-author of the cost analysis. His sentiments are echoed by other cybersecurity specialists. "I just didn't have the tools," recalls Meg King, director of the Digital Futures Project at the Woodrow Wilson International Center for Scholars, who worked on a cyberdefense bill a decade ago as a senior staff member on a House homeland security subcommittee. She now describes that bill as "too little, too late." Today her think tank has begun to offer staffers short courses in cybersecurity issues, but security researchers worry that step will not be enough.

While substantially changing the outcome of an election by hacking into voting machines is extremely unlikely because those machines and the ballot counting process are very decentralized, altering voter rolls could block people from voting. If the system is even slightly exploited, says David Becker, executive director of the Center for Election Innovation & Research, it could trigger public distrust in elections. "I think the greatest challenge that we do have is to make sure that we maintain the integrity of our election system," said Joseph Maguire, the U.S. acting director of national intelligence, during recent congressional testimony.

Because election security is so important to democracy, Norden wants Congress to fund new state offices that can act as cyber-response teams when attackers try to breach or even alter voter roll information. Yet this project is one that Republican Senate Majority Leader Mitch McConnell of Kentucky has been uninterested in pursuing, arguing that such responsibility rests with the states themselves. But the funding that state governments have allocated, along with federal assistance, to date "only scratches the surface," Becker says. Continuous election security for the future means supporting states with money to update systems that store voter information and to improve cybersecurity training, he adds. "We need to address this as an ongoing expense," Becker says.

King says one reason Capitol Hill keeps proposing solutions that fall short of the problem is high staff turnover, which means knowledge evaporates when people leave. Further, institutions that provide nonpartisan information to Congress, such as the Congressional Research Service, are stretched thin. The Office of Technology Assessment, a Congressional service that was intended to advise lawmakers on science and technology issues, was shut down in 1995. Recently representatives from both parties have begun efforts to resurrect it, but support has yet to materialize into real funding.

To get staffers to better understand the threats and how to find the right solutions to technical problems such as election security, the Wilson Center established the Congressional Cybersecurity Lab under the umbrella of King's Digital Futures Project. The lab offers weekly seminars led by technologists and runs hands-on exercises over a six-week period. After staffers complete the program, they have access to a pool of experts to advise them "without a lobbyist's perspective," King says, as well as a network of lab alumni. Knowledge gained by staffers, she adds, should let them craft more effective legislation and communicate more easily with independent cybersecurity researchers at universities and corporations.

Legislators have a vested interest in supporting more secure elections and more cybersecurity expertise on Capitol Hill, points out Kathryn Waldron, a cybersecurity researcher at the R Street Institute. As 2020 campaigns gear up, hacking attempts against politicians and their offices will likely increase, she says. "It is not just a threat to national security; it is threat to American democracy at large," Waldron says.

Why We Must Protect Voting Rights

By the Editors of *Scientific American*

I n 2021 Republican legislatures in 19 states passed 34 laws that restricted access to voting in more than a dozen different ways. And those are just the bills that succeeded; hundreds of other provisions, some still under consideration, were introduced nationwide.

"The momentum around this legislation continues," the Brennan Center for Justice, which tracks these efforts, wrote on its Web site. At least 165 restrictive voting bills were already on the docket for this year by mid-January. "These early indicators—coupled with the ongoing mobilization around the Big Lie (the same false rhetoric about voter fraud that drove [last] year's unprecedented wave of vote suppression bills)—suggest that efforts to restrict and undermine the vote will continue to be a serious threat in 2022."

The GOP has justified voting restrictions by saying that it is safeguarding elections against fraud and that certain protections against electoral bias are no longer necessary. Evidence belies this ploy to seize power by disenfranchising voters, especially minorities, who tend to vote Democratic. Voter fraud is exceedingly rare in the U.S. and hasn't increased since the 1965 Voting Rights Act. But minority suffrage has grown tremendously, and the benefits of federal oversight have persisted. Alarmed by this trend, conservative legislators and jurists began chipping away at codified voting rights decades ago. They stand to gain even more ground during this year's midterm elections if left unchecked.

While odious lies about a stolen election propelled the current wave of restrictions, the path that led to this point was laid back in 2013. In the case of *Shelby County v. Holder,* the Supreme Court dismantled a key pillar of the Voting Rights Act called "preclearance," which required jurisdictions with a history of discrimination to get Justice Department or federal court approval for any planned changes to electoral rules. Arguing that patterns of discrimination had changed, Chief Justice John Roberts wrote in the majority opinion that Congress should not use "a formula based on 40-year-old facts having no logical relation to the present day."

Desmond Ang, an expert in public policy and race at Harvard University, disagrees, saying that preclearance is as essential to civil rights today as it ever has been. According to an analysis he published in 2019, that critical provision of the Voting Rights Act alone "continued to bolster enfranchisement over four decades later," especially among minorities. So enduring were the benefits, he wrote, that "broad preventative oversight encompassing the universe of potential voting changes may be the most effective means of curbing discrimination in settings like the United States, where electoral rulemaking is highly decentralized and opaque."

In a similar vein, sociologists Nicholas Pedriana and Robin Stryker concluded in a 2017 comparative analysis that of three seminal civil rights laws passed in the 1960s—the Voting Rights Act, the Fair Housing Act and the equal employment opportunity provisions of the Civil Rights Act—the Voting Rights Act was the most successful in promoting equality. Its success depended largely on what the researchers called group-centered effects, which focus on systemic disadvantage rather than individual harm, discriminatory consequences rather than intent, and remedial group results rather than justice for individual victims or wrongdoers. Removing that statutory framework produces the opposite effect, Stryker says: highly effective, systematic suppression of minority votes.

In January the Democrats' best efforts to date to repel the current onslaught of voting restrictions—the Freedom to Vote Act and the John R. Lewis Voting Rights Advancement Act—failed in the Senate. The former would have established nationwide standards for ballot access and hindered other forms of electoral prejudice such as gerrymandering. The latter would have reversed the 2013 Supreme Court ruling on preclearance as well as another one last year, which made it harder to challenge electoral rules in court on the grounds of discrimination. The bills contained the type of broad-based, preventive strategies that have been so effective at fostering racial equality at the very core of our democratic system. Ang and Stryker lamented their demise and conceded that it's difficult not to despair in the face of intense political polarization.

For decades the Voting Rights Act enjoyed bipartisan support. No longer. Yet we must restore and expand federal oversight and jurisdiction of biased electoral rules. Until then, it is incumbent on social justice movements and everyone who cares about the most fundamental of democratic rights to keep the pressure on. As sociologist Aldon Morris wrote for us in February 2021, "when President Lyndon B. Johnson formally ended the Jim Crow era by signing the Civil Rights Act in 1964 and the Voting Rights Act in 1965, he did so because massive protests raging in the streets had forced it."

Geometry Reveals the Tricks behind Gerrymandering

By Manon Bischoff

Hardly anyone reckoned that struggling in high school to calculate the area of a triangle or the volume of a prism could be used one day to influence the outcome of an election. Geometry, however, can be a powerful tool in shaping results of an electoral contest—at least in plurality voting systems.

Designing a perfect election system for multiple parties is impossible, even with mathematical tools. But if, by and large, there are only two dominant parties, as in the U.S., things should be fairly clear-cut. The party candidate with the most votes wins, right? Anyone who has followed U.S. presidential elections in recent years knows that the reality is different. One important factor is the actual shape of the voting districts. If cleverly designed, a party that is actually losing can still gain the majority of representatives—an issue that was by no means absent in the U.S. midterm elections.

Math plays an important role in determining election outcomes, particularly for the 435 seatsin the House of Representatives. By cleverly choosing the boundaries of a congressional district, a party can enable its candidate to win even if the vote count does not fairly represent the sentiment of the voters.

Here's a highly simplified example: suppose a state consists of 50 voters, 20 of whom vote for a blue party and 30 for a red party. Voters might live in a grid pattern, as in, say, some sections of Manhattan. Suppose there are 10 north-south avenues and five east-west streets. All the red voters live on the first two avenues, the ones furthest west. The blue voters reside on the other three avenues. Now the task is to divide the voters into five electoral districts of equal size.

One could draw five vertical boundaries: Then there would be two election districts with only red voters and three with only blue voters. So the votes in that district would produce three blue party representatives and two red party ones, an accurate reflection of voters' opinions.

But if the blue party were to get its way in drawing district boundaries, they might be inclined to draw the boundaries horizontally. Then all the districts would look the same, with four red voters and six blue voters each. In this case, the blue party wins in each district, and gets all five representatives. Something similar happened in New York state in 2012: 58 percent of people there voted for the Democrats, but the party got 21 of 27 seats (five more than would have been justified if the election districts had been drawn equitably).

State legislatures and the commissions that redraw district lines, on the other hand, might make a very different (somewhat more complicated) partitioning. To do this, they could pack almost all blue voters into two districts, giving the red party a majority in the three remaining districts in which there would be three red congressmen and two blue congresswomen—although more voters gave their votes to the blue party. There are numerous examples of this in U.S. congressional races. For example, in Pennsylvania in 2012, Democrats received 51 percent of the vote, but only five of 18 seats.

The deliberate redrawing of districts to gain a majority goes by the name of gerrymandering, a portmanteau of "gerry" and "salamander." The former refers to Elbridge Gerry, the governor of Massachusetts in the early 19th century, who approved extremely odd-shaped voting districts that gave his party an advantage.

Even today, in most U.S. states, legislatures decide on the division of electoral districts about every 10 years (with the appearance of the new census). Time and again, the incumbent parties are suspected of using redistricting to their advantage. This can often be seen in strange-shaped electoral districts, similar to the one in Massachusetts at the beginning of the 19th century. A cartoonist at the time noticed that one of the districts resembled a salamander and thus coined the expression gerrymandering.

Redistricting has provoked numerous legal challenges. In 1986, the U.S. Supreme Court even ruled that intentional gerrymandering is illegal. But since then, it has barely touched an election district.

As it turns out, setting rules for fair districting is not so easy. Even mathematicians are racking their brains over the question—and arming themselves with enormous computer power to deal with the problem.

How can you find gerrymandering? Observing one Maryland district, you might suspect the designers had certain ulterior motives. What is particularly striking is that it is extremely jagged. One assertion is that district borders should be "compact"—but without defining what "compact" means exactly.

One possible clue that gerrymandering may be present is the length of the outer boundary: the more jagged a district, the larger the perimeter. The literature related to redistricting sometimes advocates drawing the smallest possible circle to include the area within a district and comparing it to the area of existing boundaries. The more the district's borders deviate from a circle, the greater the possibility that the district has been redrawn to suit partisan ends. The average distance between residents of a precinct may also indicate gerrymandering.

The partitioning into electoral districts is anything but simple. Each state follows its own rules in doing so. The ideal goal is for a district to contain roughly equal numbers of voters, be contiguous, not discriminate against ethnic groups, not cross county lines, and follow natural boundary lines, such as rivers. Such restrictions by themselves result in fractured districts—without even considering the voting behavior of residents.

A compact voting district does not necessarily lead to equitable representation, as a 2013 study found. The study paid particular attention to the 2000 presidential election in Florida, in which about as many people voted for Democrats as Republicans, but the latter accounted for 68 percent of the votes in Florida's congressional districts. The researchers used a nonpartisan algorithm designed to draw the most "compact" districts possible while adhering to the state's established rules.

Surprisingly, the computer also produced skewed results, in which Republicans would mostly have an advantage. And experts quickly realized the reason: most Democrats live in Florida cities. This means they win urban districts overwhelmingly, while narrowly losing in rural areas in each case. Because of this "natural gerrymandering," more Republicans inevitably take seats in the House of Representatives.

Florida is not an isolated case, as political scientist Jonathan A. Rodden noted. The main problem is not a district's lack of "compactness." If you want to prove that a boundary was deliberately drawn to give one party an advantage, you need more evidence than the mere shape of a district. The goal in an unbiased system is to find electoral districts so that each party has an equal chance of converting its votes into electoral seats. But how can we measure that? In 2014, University of Chicago legal scholar Nicholas Stephanopoulos and Public Policy Institute of California political scientist Eric McGhee developed a metric for the problem, the efficiency gap. It is calculated by subtracting the "wasted" votes of two parties from each other and then dividing by the total number of all votes. A wasted vote for any party, in this example, is one that ends up in a losing district that went to the opposite party or that is above the margin needed to win. The smaller the efficiency gap, the more impartial is the result.

To visualize this, we can again use the initial example with the 50 voters (20 for red, 30 for blue) and calculate the efficiency gap for the different divisions. In the first case, when all boundaries were drawn vertically, the first and second districts (from the left) each have 10 red votes, wasting four each. The third, fourth and fifth districts, on the other hand, each have 10 blue votes, four of which are also wasted. Thus, the efficiency gap is as follows (the vertical bars indicate absolute value): $|(2 \times 4) - (3 \times 4)|/50 = 2/25 = 0.08$.

In the second division, each district is equal: blue always wins by six votes out of 10. Thus, none of blue's votes are wasted—whereas all of red's are. The efficiency gap is $20/50 = 0.4$, which is significantly higher than in the first division.

The third example is the most intriguing: the two districts in which blue wins 9 to 1 each have a blue surplus of three. In the three winning red districts, four blue votes each are wasted—so in total, $(2 \times 3) + (3 \times 4) = 18$ blue votes that are surplus ones. In contrast, there are only two red votes that were wasted. This results in an efficiency gap of $(18 - 2)/50 = 8/25 = 0.32$.

The efficiency gap is useful as an indicator that pins down partisanship in voting districts. But sometimes natural conditions, such as when almost all voters of a party live in the same city, make it hard to find better possibilities. To investigate these possibilities, statistician Wendy Cho, along with computer scientist Yan Liu and geographer Shaowen Wang of the University of Illinois at Urbana-Champaign, designed an algorithm that divides maps into districts—based on the rules set by the state in question.

Finding the best possible division of districts so that each party has the same probability of converting a vote into a seat is extremely difficult. The task falls into the class of so-called NP problems, which computer scientists and mathematicians have suspected for decades cannot be solved efficiently with ordinary computers. That doesn't mean you can't find a solution—just that it may take a very, very long time. So Cho and her co-authors decided to let the computer construct an extremely large number of splits that are not necessarily perfect.

For example, when they applied their program to the state of Maryland in 2011, they realized that almost all of the 250 million results gave an advantage to Democrats. Apparently, the natural conditions, along with the requirements for voting districts, are such that Republicans are automatically at a disadvantage. Cho and her colleagues compared Maryland's actual apportionment with the computer's output and were able to show that the official voting districts favored Democrats in more than 99.79 percent of the 250 million computer-generated results.

Meanwhile, some U.S. states (mainly those where Democrats are in the majority) use independent commissions that redraw voting districts. These panels often resort to computer programs to find the fairest possible apportionment. In general, the apportionment of electoral districts this year appears to be the fairest in 40 years, as reported by the New York Times. When advantageous or detrimental districting decisions for both parties in all U.S. states are netted against one another, gerrymandering should result in only three extra seats for Republicans– down from 23 seats in 2012. But even three seats could be decisive in a close election. And news stories before the midterms depicted how gerrymandering is still very much a matter of public debate: Alabama's state legislature redistricted to put many of the Black voters in the state into just one district, decreasing their electoral power, and resulting in a case that is now before the U.S. Supreme Court.

About the Author

Manon Bischoff is a theoretical physicist and editor at Spektrum, *a partner publication of* Scientific American.

How AI Bots Could Sabotage 2024 Elections around the World

By Charlotte Hu

Hate speech, political propaganda and outright lies are hardly new problems online—even if election years such as this one exacerbate them. The use of bots, or automated social media accounts, has made it much easier to spread deliberately incorrect disinformation, as well as inaccurate rumors or other kinds of misinformation. But the bots that afflicted past voting seasons often churned out poorly constructed, grammatically incorrect sentences. Now as large language models (artificial intelligence systems that create text) become ever more accessible to more people, some researchers fear that automated social media accounts will soon get a lot more convincing.

Disinformation campaigns, online trolls and other "bad actors" are set to increasingly use generative AI to fuel election falsehoods, according to a new study published in *PNAS Nexus.* In it, researchers project that—based on "prior studies of cyber and automated algorithm attacks"—AI will help spread toxic content across social media platforms on a near-daily basis in 2024. The potential fallout, the study authors say, could affect election results in more than 50 countries holding elections this year, from India to the U.S.

This research mapped the connections between bad actor groups across 23 online platforms that included Facebook and Twitter as well as niche communities on Discord and Gab, says the study's lead author Neil Johnson, a physics professor at George Washington University. Extremist groups that post a lot of hate speech, the study found, tend to form and survive longer on smaller platforms—which generally have fewer resources for content moderation. But their messages can have a much wider reach.

Many small platforms are "incredibly well connected, to each other and internally," Johnson says. This allows disinformation to bounce like a pinball across 4chan forums and other laxly moderated websites.

If malicious content seeps out of these networks onto mainstream social sites such as YouTube, Johnson and his colleagues estimate that one billion people are potentially vulnerable to it.

"Social media lowered the cost for disseminating misinformation or information. AI is lowering the cost for producing it," says Zeve Sanderson, executive director of New York University's Center for Social Media and Politics, who was not involved in the new study. "Now, whether you're a foreign malign actor or a part of a smaller domestic campaign, you're able to use these technologies to produce multimedia content that's going to be somewhat compelling."

Studies of disinformation in previous elections have pinpointed how bots at large can spread malicious content across social media, thereby manipulating online discussions and eroding trust. In the past bots would take messages created by a person or program and repeat them, but today's large language models (LLMs) are enhancing those bots with a new feature: machine-written text that sounds convincingly human. "Generative AI alone is not more dangerous than bots. It's bots plus generative AI," says computational social scientist Kathleen Carley of Carnegie Mellon University's School of Computer Science. Generative AI and large language models can also be used to write software, making it faster and easier for programmers to code bots.

Many early bots were limited to relatively short posts, but generative AI can make realistic, paragraphs-long comments, says Yilun Du, a Ph.D. student studying generative AI modeling at the Massachusetts Institute of Technology's Computer Science & Artificial Intelligence Laboratory. Currently, AI-generated images or videos are easier to detect than text; with images and videos, Du explains, "you have to get every pixel perfect, so most of these tools are actually very inaccurate in terms of lighting or other effects on images." Text, however, is the ultimate challenge. "We don't have tools with any meaningful success rate that can identify LLM-generated texts," Sanderson says.

Still, there are some tells that *can* tip off experts to AI-generated writing: grammar that is too perfect, for example, or a lack of slang, emotional words or nuance. "Writing software that shows what is made by humans and what is not, and doing that kind of testing, is very costly and very hard," Carley says. Although her team has worked on programs to identify AI bot content on specific social media platforms, she says the tools are imperfect. And each program would have to be completely redone to function on a different website, Carley adds, because people on X (formerly Twitter), for instance, communicate in ways that are distinct from those of Facebook users.

Many experts doubt that AI detection programs—those that analyze text for the signs of a large language model's involvement—can adequately identify AI-generated content. Adding watermarks to such material, or filters and guardrails into the AI models themselves, can't cover all the bases, either. "In the area of using AI and disinformation, we're in an arms race" with bad actors, Carley says. "As soon as we come up with a way of detecting it, they come up with a way of making it better." Johnson and his colleagues also found that bad actors are likely to abuse base versions of generative AI, such as GPT-2, which are publicly available and have looser content filters than the current models. Other researchers predict that impending malicious content won't be made with big companies' sophisticated AI but instead generated by open-source tools made by a few or individual programmers.

But bots can evolve in tandem, even with these simpler versions of AI. In previous election cycles, bot networks remained near the fringe of social media. Experts predict that AI-generated disinformation will spread much more widely this time around. It's not just because AI can produce content faster; social media use dynamics have changed, too. "Up until TikTok, most of the social media that we saw were friend-, follower-, social graph-based networks. It tended to be that people followed people who they were aligned with," Sanderson explains. TikTok instead uses an algorithmic feed that injects content from accounts that users don't follow, and other platforms have altered their algorithms to follow suit. Also, as Sanderson points out, it includes topics "that the platform is trying to discover if you like or not," leading to "a much broader net of content consumption."

In Sanderson's previous studies of bots on Twitter, research assistants often labeled an account as a bot or not by looking at its account activity, including the photos and texts it posts or reposts. "It was essentially like this kind of Turing test for accounts," he says. But as AI generation gets steadily better at removing grammatical irregularities and other signifiers of bot content, Sanderson believes that the responsibility of identifying these accounts will have to fall to social media companies. These companies have the ability to check metadata associated with the accounts, to which external researchers rarely have access.

Rather than going after false content itself, some disinformation experts think that finding and containing the people who make it would be a more practical approach. Effective countermeasures, Du suggests, could function by detecting activity from certain IP addresses or identifying when there's a suspiciously large number of posts at a certain time of day.

This could potentially work because there are "fewer bad actors than bad content," Carley says. And disinformation peddlers are concentrated in certain corners of the Internet. "We know that a bunch of the stuff comes from a few main websites that link to each other, and the content of those websites is generated by LLMs," she adds. "If we can detect the bad website as a whole, we've suddenly captured tons of bad information." Additionally, Carley and Johnson agree that moderating content at the level of small social media communities (posts by members of specific Facebook pages or Telegram channels, for instance) would be more effective than sweeping policies that ban entire categories of content.

Not all is lost to the bots yet, however. Despite reasonable concerns about AI's impact on elections, Sanderson and his colleagues recently argued against overstating potential harms. The actual effects of increased AI content and bot activity on human behaviors—including polarization, vote choice and cohesion—still need more research. "The fear I have is that we're going to spend so much time trying to identify that something is happening and assume that we know the effect," Sanderson says. "It could be the case that the effect isn't that large, and the largest effect is the fear of it, so we end up just eroding trust in the information ecosystem."

About the Author

Charlotte Hu is a science and technology journalist based in Brooklyn, N.Y. She's interested in stories at the intersection of science and society. Her work has appeared in Popular Science, GenomeWeb, Business Insider *and* Discover *magazine.*

Section 5: Politics Meets Science Policy

A Plan to Defend against
the War on Science

By Shawn Otto

F our years ago in *Scientific American*, I warned readers of a
growing problem in American democracy. The article, entitled
"Antiscience Beliefs Jeopardize U.S. Democracy," charted how it
had not only become acceptable, but often required, for politicians
to embrace antiscience positions, and how those positions flew
in the face of the core principles that the U.S. was founded on:
That if anyone could discover the truth of something for him or
herself using the tools of science, then no king, no pope and no
wealthy lord was more entitled to govern the people than they
were themselves. It was self-evident.

In the years since, the situation has gotten worse. We've seen
the emergence of a "post-fact" politics, which has normalized the
denial of scientific evidence that conflicts with the political, religious
or economic agendas of authority. Much of this denial centers, now
somewhat predictably, around climate change—but not all. If there
is a single factor to consider as a barometer that evokes all others
in this election, it is the candidates' attitudes toward science.

Consider, for example, what has been occurring in Congress. Rep.
Lamar Smith, the Texas Republican who chairs the House Committee
on Science, Space and Technology, is a climate change denier.
Smith has used his post to initiate a series of McCarthy-style witch-
hunts, issuing subpoenas and demanding private correspondence
and testimony from scientists, civil servants, government science
agencies, attorneys general and nonprofit organizations whose work
shows that global warming is happening, humans are causing it and
that—surprise—energy companies sought to sow doubt about this fact.

Smith, who is a Christian Scientist and seems to revel in his role
as the science community's bête noire, is by no means alone. Climate
denial has become a virtual Republican Party plank (and rejecting the

Paris climate accord a literal one) with a wide majority of Congressional Republicans espousing it. Sen. Ted Cruz (R–Texas), chairman of the Senate's Subcommittee on Space, Science and Competitiveness, took time off from his presidential campaign last December to hold hearings during the Paris climate summit showcasing well-known climate deniers repeating scientifically discredited talking points.

The situation around science has grown so partisan that Hillary Clinton turned the phrase "I believe in science" into the largest applause line of her convention speech accepting the Democratic Party nomination. Donald Trump, by contrast, is the first major party presidential nominee who is an outright climate denier, having called climate science a "hoax" numerous times. In his responses to the organization I helped found, ScienceDebate.org, which gets presidential candidates on the record on science, he told us that "there is still much that needs to be investigated in the field of 'climate change,'" putting the term in scare quotes to cast doubt on its reality. When challenged on his hoax comments, campaign manager Kellyanne Conway affirmed that Trump doesn't believe climate change is man-made.

Over the last 25 years the political right has largely organized itself along antiscience lines that have become increasingly stark: fundamentalist evangelicals, who reject what the biological sciences have to say about human origins, sexuality and reproduction, serve as willing foot soldiers for moneyed business interests who reject what the environmental sciences have to say about pollution and resource extraction. In 1990, for example, House Democrats scored an average of 68 percent on the League of Conservation Voters National Environmental Scorecard and Republicans scored a respectable 40 percent. But by 2014 Democrats scored 87 percent whereas Republican scores fell to just over 4 percent.

Such rejection is essentially an authoritarian argument that says "I don't care about the evidence; what I say/what this book says/ what my tribe says/what my wallet says goes." This approach is all too human, and is not necessarily conscious. It is, rather, reflective of the sort of confirmation bias scientists themselves continually guard against. Francis Bacon noted the problem at the beginning of the scientific revolution, observing: "What a man had rather were true he more readily believes." Conservatives notice that many scientists are, in fact, left-leaning. If one is not a scientist, and is conservative, a shorthand is brought to bear, with suspicion of the science as—rather than an objective statement—being a politically motivated argument from the left.

Those on the left are more inclined to accept the evidentiary conclusions from biological and environmental science but they are not immune to antiscience attitudes themselves. There, scientifically discredited fears that vaccines cause autism have led to a liberal anti-vaccination movement, endangering public health. Fears that GMO (genetically modified) food is unsafe to eat, equally unsupported, propel a national labeling movement. Fears that cell phones cause brain cancer or wi-fi causes health problems or water fluoridation can lower IQ, none supported by science, also largely originate from the political left.

Much of this comes from suspicions of so-called regulatory capture, in which government agencies align themselves with corporate interests, a danger the Green Party candidate, Jill Stein, raised in her answer to ScienceDebate.org about vaccination. These suspicions are not always unfounded, and if one can't trust the impartiality of government safety regulations, the avoidance principle becomes the default position and science is denied on the basis that it's corporate PR. This was well illustrated by a 2011 battle in San Francisco, where the board of supervisors, all of them Democrats, voted 10–1 to require cell phone shops to warn customers that they may cause brain cancer (an ordinance that was widely criticized and later repealed). The difference is that although those on the left seek to extend regulations based on fears that are not always supported by science, those on the right oppose regulations that are.

Such confirmation bias has been enabled by a generation of university academics who have taught a corrosive brand of postmodernist identity politics that argues truth is relative, and that science is a "meta-narrative"—a story concocted by the ruling white male elite in order to retain power—and therefore suspect. The claims of science, these academics argue, are no more privileged than any other "way of knowing," such as black truth, female truth or indigenous truth. We can't know, a Minneapolis professor recently argued, that Earth goes around the sun, for example, because these sorts of worldviews have been dislodged by paradigm shifts throughout history. Thus, each of us constructs our own truth, and the job of an educator or a journalist is to facilitate that process of discovery.

The ideas of postmodernism align well with the identity politics of the left, and they have helped to empower disadvantaged voices, which always adds to the conversation. But what works in this case for political discourse is demonstrably false when applied to science. A scientific statement stands independent of the gender, sexual orientation, ethic background, religion or political identity of the person taking the measurement. That's the whole point. It's tied to the object being measured, not the subject doing the measuring.

By undermining science's claim of objectivity, these postmodernists have unwittingly laid the philosophical foundation for the new rise of authoritarianism. Because if there is no objective evidence that has ultimate credibility, how is one to settle competing claims of truth, such as those made by Trump? Without objective truth, the nattering of warring pundits can go on forever, and can only be settled by those with the biggest stick or the loudest megaphone—in short, by authoritarian assertion, a situation not of postmodernism but of premodernism. Which is exactly what's happening. And which runs completely counter to the enlightenment ideas of American democracy and the journalism that is supposed to inform it.

The problem is that the dangers science is revealing are real, and the failure to regulate, promoted in the name of free market economics, is itself scientifically unsupported. The exploding human population coupled with expanding technological power is having a profound collective impact on a nonexpanding planet. When Adam Smith first offered the libertarian idea of the self-regulating market's "invisible hand," the world was effectively unlimited, and relying only on market forces to produce the highest good seemed reasonable because one was never concerned with waste that wouldn't flow away or resources that wouldn't replenish.

But the model becomes a problem when the world is limited, population has grown exponentially, we are swimming in waste and facing dwindling resources, and our cumulative exhaust is warming the planet. These are scientific facts, and facing them implies regulation of the free market. It's no surprise, then, that the science has divided along political lines between those on the left, who favor personal morality and collective responsibility via regulation and those on the right who favor collective morality and personal responsibility through regulation's removal.

Industry's war against science isn't limited to climate change. A host of public relations campaigns over the last five decades have spent billions of dollars with the express purpose of sowing public doubt about science. The techniques are usually the same: highlight cherry-picked facts provided by paid physicians or scientists whose alternative conclusions support your agenda; emphasize the need for healthy debate (when there really is none); attack the integrity of mainstream science and scientists; emphasize the negative consequences of tackling the problem; feed stories to sympathetic journalists (or purchase a news outlet); fund "Astroturf" groups to create the illusion of grassroots support; call for "balance"; and give money to lawmakers who will vote your way.

In the 1960s tobacco, for example, companies mounted a campaign to create public uncertainty about the scientific evidence that smoking causes cancer. The sugar industry funded research at Harvard University for decades to create uncertainty about sugar's role in heart disease while promoting fat as the real culprit. The chemical industry vilified Rachel Carson to create uncertainty about the environmental problems caused by pesticides. The construction and resource extraction industries paid consultants to help them create uncertainty about the health risks of asbestos, silica and lead. More recently the National Football League used incomplete data and league-affiliated doctors to create uncertainty about the relationship between head trauma and chronic traumatic encephalopathy. The central message is always: because we can't be 100 percent certain, we should do nothing.

The partisan split has been exacerbated by these campaigns, and by a news media that has been trained for two generations in the false postmodernist view that there is no such thing as objectivity. Journalism schools teach it; it's contained in reporter guidelines and repeated by leading journalists. Intended as an admonishment against assuming one's own reporting is unbiased, the mantra has become so ingrained that reporters rarely challenge those in power on evidentiary grounds, which is one of the main purposes of the fourth estate. David Gregory, NBC News's chief White House correspondent during the George W. Bush administration, put it quite clearly in his defense of the White House press corps for not pushing Pres. Bush on the lack of credible evidence of Saddam Hussein's "weapons of mass destruction" before the U.S. invaded Iraq. "I think there are a lot of critics who think that...if we did not stand up and say this is bogus, and you're a liar, and why are you doing this, that we didn't do our job," Gregory said. "I respectfully disagree. It's not our role."

But if it is not the press's role, whose is it? Is it partisan to challenge Trump on his false assertions about global warming? How are people to make well-informed decisions about momentous policies or important elections without accurate, reasonably objective information and questioning of the powerful? Instead, journalists often seek to find stand-ins who will provide opposing arguments and create "balance," so they can appear as neutral arbiters in a playground spat. But the journalistic principle of balance gets into trouble when there is a matter in which significant evidence from science can be brought to bear.

Public relations firms know this and take advantage of it to manipulate journalists. A journalist who dedicates half the story to a scientist who is representing all the knowledge created from tens of thousand of experiments carried out by thousands of scientists (many of whom have risked their careers and sometimes their lives) using billions of data points, on the one hand; and the other half to a passionate advocate with an opposing opinion representing a minority view or from outside of science altogether, is engaging in false balance. Such representations portray the outlier views as if they have the same weight as those of the mainstream science, and thus elevate extreme views (and extreme partisanship) in the national dialogue.

The authoritarian nature of science denial is part and parcel of the rise of a new authoritarian nationalism that is in reaction to the globalization brought about by our postwar scientific success, and is antithetical to science and the scientific process of investigation. Such authoritarians put science in their crosshairs and claim it is a partisan tool, just as they have argued against the "liberal media" to cow journalists from testing claims against evidence. But science is never partisan. To be effective, scientists must be both conservative and progressive: They must survey all the known science on a given topic and at least acknowledge and account for those traditional values if they publish something new on the topic or they risk career suicide.

But they must also be open to new insights and new ways of thinking, because that's where the frontier is, and to do less is to risk career stagnation, another form of suicide. Science is never partisan but it is inherently political, because its antiauthoritarian, evidence-based conclusions either confirm or challenge somebody's cherished ideological or economic interests—and that is always political. Considered this way, politics is not a simple left-right continuum; it also has a vertical component between authoritarianism and antiauthoritarianism. Thus there are authoritarians like Mao and Stalin on the left; Hitler and Mussolini on the right, but what they have in common is intolerance to the sort of open exchange that is central to art, science, and human progress.

This vertical tension between experts and authoritarians helps explain what is going on in both the Republican Party and in the European Union with the Brexit vote and the rise of a new authoritarianism, and why it is so corrosive to science. The argument is between antiauthoritarians who support science and evidence, and authoritarians who have had enough of experts.

This problem can be expected to worsen in the coming years, particularly if authoritarian candidates continue to be elected with the aid of a news media that treats any view, no matter how unsupported, as legitimate. We are creating knowledge at 10 times the rate we have in the recent past. All of that new information must be parsed and its implications worked through our moral and ethical discussion, then codified in our legal and regulatory systems, and that is inevitably a fraught and political process. Advances in gene editing are providing increasing control over the process of life design and creation, raising complex ethical and political issues. Advances in neuroscience are increasingly showing the mind to be a construction of the brain.

These insights, combined with advances in pharmaceuticals and computer–brain interface technology, will challenge our ideas about psychology, spirituality and personal responsibility as well as upend our ideas about criminal justice. And yet we are still stuck in a 40-year debate over the evidence that humans are causing global warming.

There are solutions, however. Sciencedebate.org is certainly a start. Evidence shows the public is hungry for such discussion of science-driven issues—which affect voters at least as much as the economics, foreign policy, and faith and values issues candidates traditionally discuss—that afford an opportunity to hold candidates to account on the evidence. Individuals can join and support organizations like ScienceDebate.org or the Union of Concerned Scientists that fight for scientific integrity. Pastors and preachers can certainly do more by staying informed of cutting-edge science and helping their parishioners parse the complex moral and ethical implications of new knowledge instead of rehashing old political divides. Educators can develop model curricula and provide training for science-civics classes at the secondary and postsecondary level so that nonscience students develop an understanding of how science works in public policy as well as how it relates to their daily lives. There are dozens of others. I discuss many of these solutions in my new book, *The War on Science*.

"Wherever the people are well informed," Thomas Jefferson wrote, "they can be trusted with their own government." We have to develop more robust ways of incorporating rapidly advancing scientific knowledge into our political dialogue, so that voters can continue to guide the democratic process and battle back authoritarianism as we did at our foundation and have done throughout our history. That will require the media to rethink their role in reporting on issues in which scientific knowledge is crucial. Is that idealistic? Yes. But so were America's founders.

About the Author

Shawn Otto (http://shawnotto.com) is the award-winning author of The War on Science: Who's Waging It, Why It Matters, What We Can Do About It *(https://www.amazon.com/War-Science-Waging-Matters-About/dp/1571313532). He is cofounder and chair of ScienceDebate.org.* Scientific American *is media partner to the ScienceDebate project.*

Yes, Science Is Political

By Alyssa Shearer, Ingrid Joylyn Paredes,
Tiara Ahmad and Christopher Jackson

S cience isn't political."
If you're in STEM, you've likely heard this refrain before; its sentiment might even resonate with you. It may not surprise you that only 43.6 percent of STEM students voted in the last presidential election, compared to 49.2 and 53.2 percent of students in the humanities and social sciences, respectively.

Science, however, has always been political; the events of 2020 have only made the relationship between science and society more explicit. We are in the midst of a pandemic and a climate crisis, both solvable by centering scientific expertise. When our government ignores scientists, the consequences can be fatal, disproportionately so for Black, brown and Indigenous communities. Americans are suffering from wildfire-induced poor air quality. More than 200,000 Americans have died from COVID-19. Yet, as our nation grapples with the pandemic, our current administration believes that "science shouldn't stand in the way" of business as usual.

We cannot accept this. Now is the time for science, not silence. In November, we scientists must vote for an administration that allows science to lead the way in the formation of policy.

As scientists, we're trained to think of the broader impacts of our research; as citizens, we should make those thoughts concrete with our votes. We have been trained to think critically, analyze large amounts of data and come up with potential solutions to the problems we discover. We can use these same skills to analyze policy, and we must, because doing so promotes an informed citizenry. Various examples of scientists who did just this exist in our history. Albert Einstein was an outspoken antiwar activist. Andrei Sakharov fought against nuclear proliferation.

Women, in particular, have long been leaders in the environmental movement; Rachel Carson wrote *Silent Spring*, sparking the contemporary environmental movement in the United States. Wangari Maathai worked tirelessly throughout her life in many humanitarian efforts, including founding the Green Belt Movement. These scientists made a societal impact by bringing their knowledge and expertise outside of the lab. And today, scientist-activists including Dior Vargas, Ayana Elizabeth Johnson and Geoffrey Supran have continued this legacy, advocating for science and science-based policies.

The classroom can be a starting point to encourage STEM students and scientists to become more civically engaged. Just as we discuss problem sets, we should discuss how scientific advancements affect society, such as the potential benefits and dangers of unregulated facial recognition software and using CRISPR gene editing technology for therapeutic purposes. Lessons should be taught on how science can be grounded in justice, such as in agroecology, which is used for both sustainable farming and to promote a more just food system. Likewise, science classes should highlight current events in politics that influence scientific data production and usage. The current administration has censored climate scientists. Until recently, scientists could not use federal funding to study gun violence, which is widely recognized as a public health crisis. And of course, policies have real impact on our lives: immigration bans jeopardize the collaborative nature of scientific research and instead foster fear and uncertainty in researchers. If you can vote, use your voice to support candidates and policies that prioritize using science for our common good.

Below we have compiled suggestions that universities, educators and students can use to increase STEM voter turnout this fall and beyond.

For university administrators:

- Make election days a university holiday so that all students, faculty, and staff have the opportunity to vote in person.
- Use classrooms and auditorium spaces for polling, which will increase the accessibility of voting to students.

For educators:

- Include information about voter registration on your syllabus.
- Remind students of voter registration deadlines. Whether you have five minutes or a full class period, the Union of Concerned Scientists has shared resources on how to bring democracy into the classroom.
- Structure the course schedule with election days in mind: don't plan exams, project due dates or mandatory participation activities for election week, to allow students ample time to vote in potentially long lines and not sacrifice important study time.
- Incorporate discussions tying science to society. March for Science NYC curated a panel series connecting science to voter issues.
- Discuss the work that scientists have done as activists in your field.

For students:

- Organize your friends, classmates and STEM co-workers: register to vote and make a voting plan together.
- Hold a voter registration drive targeting STEM communities on campus.
- Join or start an organization that focuses on science community building. Examples include 500 Women Scientists, Black in the Ivory and 500 Queer Scientists.
- Attend or host a science and society lecture and discussion event to highlight how science can be used in policy.
- Volunteer in your community with local citizen science groups, your local government, or advocacy organizations.
- Whatever cause you are already passionate about—animal rights, the environment, world hunger, patient advocacy—learn how science relates and how policies can use this science to create effective solutions.

In short, as Rosalind Franklin, whom many think deserved to share the Nobel Prize for her role in elucidating the structure of

DNA, said, "Science and everyday life cannot and should not be separated." For us scientists and citizens, we must advocate for science. Our world is facing a life-threatening climate crisis and a neglected pandemic, and is reckoning with centuries of unjust systems. We need to organize and vote like it.

About the Authors

Alyssa Shearer is a science educator and a team leader of March for Science NYC.

Ingrid Joylyn Paredes is a Ph.D. candidate in chemical engineering at New York University.

Tiara Ahmad received her Ph.D. in pathology and molecular medicine from Columbia University.

Christopher Jackson is a Ph.D. candidate in chemistry at the University of California, Berkeley.

On Election Day, Vote for Candidates with Science-Based Policies, Not Politicians Who Ignore Evidence

By the Editors of *Scientific American*

E lections have consequences," said President Barack Obama in 2009, as he started to press for policies such as affordable health care against Republican opposition. Recently Republican leaders themselves have begun to echo his phrase as red state legislatures ban abortion, prevent the country from taking actions to combat the climate crisis, permit easier access to firearms, and oppose a vigorous public health response to the pandemic. All of that makes the consequences of this fall's vote exceptionally profound.

What these issues have in common is overwhelming scientific support for pursuing one policy direction over another. They share something else, too: a choice between candidates who either follow that scientific evidence or act as if it does not exist. On your Election Day ballot you'll see local and federal candidates who endorse policies based on tested scientific evidence and others who take positions based on unsupported assumptions and biases. The scientific method has brought us vaccines, the Internet, cleaner air and water, and entire new sectors of the economy. Office seekers who use research-based evidence to inform decisions are the ones who will help our country prosper. Those who reject this evidence will increase suffering. The following survey of urgent policy issues highlights the differences:

Reproductive and gender rights. When the Supreme Court overturned Roe v. Wade and allowed any state to ban or restrict abortion rights, it let those states force people to undergo the risk of pregnancy against their will. About 50 scientific papers have compared women who received an abortion when they wanted one with women who were turned away. The women denied abortion, followed for several years, had worse physical and mental health. They were also more likely to live below the federal poverty level and be unemployed. Pregnancy itself is far more dangerous than abortion. The U.S. already has a startlingly high rate of maternal mortality, and one study estimates that a national ban would drive up those deaths by 21 percent. Office seekers who support abortion bans ignore such evidence; instead many favor narrow religious doctrine.

Politicians who oppose gender-affirming health care are just as blinkered. Alabama enacted a law criminalizing such care for transgender youth while Texas directed state officials to investigate such care as child abuse. Florida wants the treatments withheld. These positions ignore the lifesaving effects of these treatments. A 2020 study in the journal *Pediatrics* looked at teenagers who were denied hormone-blocking treatments that temporarily delay puberty while the youth consider their gender. Those teens went on to have a much greater lifetime risk of suicidal thoughts. The effects of this medication are reversible.

Health and the pandemic. This summer Congress passed a budget bill with several key health-care provisions. One was to give Medicare the power to negotiate wildly escalating drug prices with pharmaceutical manufacturers. More than 47 percent of new drugs released in 2020–2021 cost more than $150,000 a year, according to a study in the journal *JAMA*; only 9 percent of new drugs topped that dollar figure as recently as 2013. The bill will put more lifesaving medications in the hands of more Americans, yet Senate Republicans opposed it. They eliminated a specific provision to cap the cost of insulin at $35 per month for people with private insurance. Right now in the U.S., a single dose can cost more than $300, forcing many of the several million Americans with type 1 diabetes to skip doses. And the evidence is clear that affordable health care saves lives. One study showed that states that expanded eligibility for Medicaid, a low-cost health program, saved thousands of people from premature deaths. States that voted against such expansion went in the opposite direction, and people lost years of life.

The U.S. pandemic response has been filled with missteps on all sides. But many conservative Republican-led jurisdictions have been exceptionally hostile to basic public health measures. Despite the large number of studies showing masks reduce transmission of the SARS-CoV-2 virus (the N95 style is the most effective version), these places resisted mask mandates, even as the U.S. climbed to a nationwide toll of more than one million deaths from COVID. Several Republican-led state legislatures introduced laws that took power away from local public health agencies and gave it to state politicians. And officials in Florida, urged on by Governor Ron DeSantis, refused to recommend COVID vaccines for any children or teens. At that time, 1,200 children nationwide had been killed by the virus, and a study had shown vaccines were 94 percent effective at keeping kids aged 12 through 18 out of the hospital. None of the clinical trials of vaccines in children found serious adverse health events.

Gun safety. In the U.S., we are dying from a plague of gunfire: 45,000 people are killed by firearms every year; the most recent numbers show more children and young adults were killed by guns than by cars. While the pace of mass shootings in 2022—at least one incident a day where at least four people were killed or injured—grabs headlines, most of the thousands of victims are shot one or two at a time. The death toll disproportionately hits people of color. Just more than half of the dead are Black men. And deaths do not capture the entire grim story. Approximately 85,000 people were wounded by gunfire in 2017, the most recent year for which these data are available; many of them have pain and disability for the rest of their lives. Still, many politicians, supported by pro-gun lobby groups, want to relax permit rules and make these weapons of mass destruction easier to get.

One false claim repeatedly made by these officials is that more armed good guys will stop more armed bad guys. Senator Ted Cruz of Texas used this disproven refrain after the school massacre in Uvalde, where in fact many armed good guys (the police) did not stop one bad guy. More to the point, research carried out by investigators at Texas State University using FBI data showed that an armed bystander shot the attacker only 22 times out of 433 active shooter incidents. Even when a "good guy" has a weapon, the carnage is already done. For instance, in a Sutherland Springs, Tex., church shooting, an armed neighbor fired at the assailant but only after 25 people had been killed, including a pregnant woman, and 22 wounded.

When guns are in a home, not out on the street, the research clearly shows that more firearms mean more death and crime. A 2003 study looked at levels of gun ownership among murder and suicide victims. Among gun owners, the odds of becoming a murder victim were 41 percent higher when compared with people who did not keep guns in the house. The odds for dying by suicide were 244 percent higher. That last tragic number is important: of those 45,000 annual firearm-related deaths, nearly 25,000 are suicides.

There are ways to improve gun safety and save innocent lives. These approaches have been studied and demonstrated, and candidates who support them deserve votes. Safe firearm-storage laws should be passed and enforced, for instance. Stricter regulation of gun dealers is an effective measure, as are universal background checks, mandatory licensing requirements, red flag laws, and bans on assault-style weapons and magazines that hold enormous amounts of bullets.

Climate. After being chopped down from trillions to billions of dollars in spending, the Biden administration's climate bill passed, and it does have some significant wins. Chief among them: support for solar panels and wind turbines and funds for clean energy projects in poor communities. But on the state level, some Republican-dominated legislatures are throwing up obstacles to cuts in fossil-fuel use. These reductions, according to scientific consensus, are needed to stop the temperature rise that's driving catastrophic storms, droughts, floods and wildfires in the U.S. Yet West Virginia's attorney general announced plans to sue the federal government if it rules that publicly traded companies have to reveal their levels of greenhouse gas emissions. Several Republican state lawmakers have introduced bills to punish companies if they divest from fossil fuels. And Texas passed a law prohibiting new construction that avoids natural gas as a fuel source.

There are other crucial issues that divide candidates, such as backing state bills that prevent schools from teaching about racism and sexism in American history. Promises to reduce inflation will also get a lot of attention. Take a hard look at these office seekers and their attitudes about policies based on scientific evidence. And then, we urge you, vote for science.

More Scientists Need to Run for Office. This Advocacy Group Is Teaching Them How

By Shaughnessy Naughton

M idterm elections are almost here. Most of the conversation concerns Congress and governorships, but some of the most critical and underappreciated races affect people's day-to-day lives. Positions like township supervisor, school board member or county commissioner are some of the more than 500,000 state and municipal offices in the United States that oversee complex policy, including on science-related issues including climate change, health care and reproductive choice. State-level positions spend $3.2 trillion in taxpayer funds each year, and many are held by people who deny facts, data and even reality itself when crafting policy.

In the current environment of school boards banning books, municipal leaders eschewing best public health practices, and state leaders enacting extreme abortion bans, STEM professionals and data-driven policy makers can and should run for local office. Many of these positions are not full-time; a science-driven professional can be a public servant while continuing their career as an engineer, a biology professor or physician. There is almost no issue facing our country that wouldn't benefit by having more data-driven policy makers in public service.

That's why the organization I founded, 314 Action, has put out the call for scientists to run for state and municipal offices. The time to think about running is now—to think of science in the pursuit of service. We offer tools to match your interests with an appropriate elected office. We walk you through different steps of the election process, whether when you are choosing a treasurer and filing your intent-to-run paperwork, or as you communicate with voters and organize your volunteers. For a first-time candidate, the process can seem daunting, and our tool breaks it down into a step-by-step process that is simple to follow and bring to success.

In addition to building our community of scientist donors, 314 Action has become a campaign incubator for scientists running for office. One of the first initiatives of the organization was to organize candidate trainings, teaching scientists how to successfully launch a campaign and communicate their message. And we just launched a new effort to help get scientists off the sidelines and into state legislatures and municipal offices.

While the debate among the scientific community about how much scientists should be involved in politics isn't new, the need for a support system for STEM candidates to get off the sidelines is needed now, more than ever.

I should know.

When I ran for Congress, I knew how to be a chemist, but I didn't know much about being a candidate for public office. It was 2014, and Congress was voting for the umpteenth time to repeal the Affordable Care Act, rather than working to make health care more accessible and affordable. Gun violence continued to take over 40,000 American lives a year, and yet Congress had all but banned the Centers for Disease Control and Prevention from even compiling data on gun violence. And even though climate change was recognized as a clear threat by our military and scientific establishments, many politicians were still campaigning on their skepticism.

What became apparent to me was that these weren't problems that science alone could solve. Science already told us to look to the data, and that CO_2 emissions needed to be reduced. This was a problem that only changing the policy makers and their priorities could hope to address.

Although I didn't win my race, what I learned was that it takes more than passion to succeed in electoral politics. You need a network. You need campaign expertise. You need someone to show you how to convert your analytical skills into successful campaigning.

Having a STEM leader in elected office can move the needle and give context, reasoning and a qualified argument for policy based on evidence instead of ignorance or conjecture. Examples of this at the state and municipal levels abound.

In California, state assemblymember Luz Rivas is an electrical engineer and serves as chair of Natural Resources Committee. She introduced and passed legislation to establish an advanced warning and ranking system for heat, similar to what exists for wildfires and tornadoes.

Val Arkoosh, MD, MPH is the chair of the Montgomery County Commissioners in Pennsylvania. She has used her position and expertise to systematically and equitably approach the distribution of Pandemic Recovery Funds to increase affordable housing, access to child care, the protection of open space and expand behavioral health operations and facilities.

And Andrew Zwicker, a New Jersey State Senator who holds a PhD in physics and who first won office to the State House in 2015, has sponsored several bills that were made into law that make it more simple for people to vote and participate in democracy within his state.

Of course, running for office isn't for everyone. Taking the leap is hard work—especially if you come from the hard sciences, where many of us learn little about policy and public service and the role of science in shaping society. Recognizing that we all have a civic responsibility means taking the first step: attend a school board meeting, serve on a community board, volunteer on a campaign, vote.

This isn't a novel concept when you consider the culture of support that is built into some other professions. For example, law firms traditionally support their associates when one of them runs for public office because law influences policy and policy influences law. Yet, so does science, or at least it should, but scientists and scientific careers don't have that type of culture. While we work on changing that, for scientists who are ready to take that leap, we're ready to help. And for Americans who want a policymaking system that values science and expertise, we're eager for you to join us in this fight by supporting our work.

The future of our country—and our planet—depends on it.

This is an opinion and analysis article, and the views expressed by the author or authors are not necessarily those of Scientific American.

About the Author

Shaughnessy Naughton is the president and founder of 314 Action, the largest pro-science advocacy organization committed to electing scientists to public office.

GLOSSARY

armchair diagnosis An attempt to diagnose someone with an illness without the relevant knowledge or expertise.

audit An official inspection with the purpose of avoiding corruption or mishandling.

autocratic Ruling with absolute power, or generally being domineering and forceful.

bête noire A person who is especially reviled.

confirmation bias A logical fallacy whereby someone interprets evidence only in a way to support their pre-formed conclusion.

consensus A state of shared agreement on a particular issue arrived at by a particular group.

defamation Damaging someone's reputation with untrue statements.

determinant An element that plays a role in causing or shaping an outcome.

disenfranchise To deprive of the right to vote or participate in the democratic process.

disincentivize To discourage an action, often accidentally, by removing an incentive or reason for doing it.

gatekeeper Someone with the ability to control access to something.

heuristic A cognitive strategy for easy memorization or application of information.

idealized Remembered or represented as better than it actually is.

interface In computers or other technology, the point of human interaction and control.

machination A plot or conspiracy.

mitigate To reduce the negative effects of something.

municipal Relating to the government of a city or town.

objective Rooted in truth, rather than personal opinion.

paper trail A written record of something used as evidence.

plurality The highest number of votes, whether or not it is the majority.

polling place The physical location where voting occurs.

populist A political style that claims legitimacy by representing "the people."

proprietary Owned by a person or organization, rather than freely available.

redistricting The process of redrawing voter district lines, with significant impacts on people's political representation.

relative Finding its meaning or definition only in relation to something else.

tacit Silent or unstated.

veracity Truthfulness or accuracy.

working paper An initial report of a research study that has not yet been fully edited or published.

FURTHER INFORMATION

"Poll Worker Resources for Voters," United States Election Assistance Commision, February 1, 2024, https://www.eac.gov/help-america-vote.

"Public Opinion Polling Basics," Pew Research Center, https://www.pewresearch.org/course/public-opinion-polling-basics/.

Ceci, Stephen J., and Wendy M. Williams. "The Psychology of Fact-Checking," *Scientific American*, October 25, 2020, https://www.scientificamerican.com/article/the-psychology-of-fact-checking1/.

Goldenberg, Amit. "Extreme Views Are More Attractive than Moderate Ones." *Scientific American*, April 19, 2023, https://www.scientificamerican.com/article/extreme-views-are-more-attractive-than-moderate-ones/.

Herre, Bastian. "The World Has Recently Become Less Democratic," *Our World In Data*, September 6, 2022, https://ourworldindata.org/less-democratic.

Murtagh, Jack. "The Strangely Serious Implications of Math's 'Ham Sandwich Theorem,'" *Scientific American*, February 17, 2024, https://www.scientificamerican.com/article/the-strangely-serious-implications-of-maths-ham-sandwich-theorem/.

Shermer, Michael. "Science Denial versus Science Pleasure," *Scientific American*, September 1, 2018, https://www.scientificamerican.com/article/science-denial-versus-science-pleasure/.

Tufekci, Zeynep. "Online Voting Seems like a Great Idea—Until You Look Closer," *Scientific American*, June 1, 2019, https://www.scientificamerican.com/article/online-voting-seems-like-a-great-idea-until-you-look-closer/.

CITATIONS

1.1 The Problems with Poor Ballot Design by Catherine Caruso (November 7, 2016); 1.2 Are Blockchains the Answer for Secure Elections? Probably Not by Jesse Dunietz (August 16, 2018); 1.3 The Vulnerabilities of Our Voting Machines by Jen Schwartz (November 1, 2018); 1.4 How Medical Systems Can Help People Vote by Ilan Shapiro, Shweta Namjoshi & Olivia S. Morris (November 6, 2022); 1.5 Citizens' Assemblies Are Upgrading Democracy: Fair Algorithms Are Part of the Program by Ariel Procaccia (November 1, 2022); 1.6 Could Math Design the Perfect Electoral System? by Jack Murtagh (November 2, 2023); 2.1 Presidential Debates Have Shockingly Little Effect on Election Outcomes by Rachel Nuwer (October 20, 2022); 2.2 How the Best Forecasters Predict Events Such as Election Outcomes by Pavel Atanasov (October 20, 2020); 2.3 Why Polls Were Mostly Wrong by Gloria Dickie (November 13, 2020); 2.4 The Secret Sauce in Opinion Polling Can Also Be a Source of Spoilage by Xiao-Li Meng (December 6, 2020); 2.5 How Coin Flipping Can Make Polls More Accurate by Dennis Shasha (March 9, 2022); 3.1 Would You Vote for a Psychopath? by Kevin Dutton (September 1, 2016); 3.2 Donald Trump and the Psychology of Doom and Gloom by Anne Marthe van der Bles & Sander van der Linden (September 5, 2017); 3.3 Are Toxic Political Conversations Changing How We Feel about Objective Truth? by Matthew Fisher, Joshua Knobe, Brent Strickland & Frank C. Keil (January 2, 2018)' 3.4 Psychological Weapons of Mass Persuasion by Sander van der Linden (April 10, 2018); 3.5 The Science of America's Dueling Political Narratives by Laura Akers (October 3, 2020); 3.6 Conservative and Liberal Brains Might Have Some Real Differences by Lydia Denworth (October 26, 2020); 4.1 How Misinformation Spreads— and Why We Trust It by Cailin O'Connor & James Owen Weatherall (September 1, 2019); 4.2 Smartphone Data Show Voters in Black Neighborhoods Wait Longer by Daniel Garisto (October 1, 2019); 4.3 Congressional Ignorance Leaves the U.S. Vulnerable to Cyberthreats by Jackson Barnett (October 21, 2019); 4.4 Why We Must Protect Voting Rights by the Editors of Scientific American (April 1, 2022); 4.5 Geometry Reveals the Tricks behind Gerrymandering by Manon Bischoff (November 10, 2022); 4.6 How AI Bots Could Sabotage 2024 Elections around the World by Charlotte Hu (February 13, 2024); 5.1 A Plan to Defend against the War on Science by Shawn Otto (October 9, 2016); 5.2 Yes, Science Is Political by Alyssa Shearer, Ingrid Joylyn Paredes, Tiara Ahmad & Christopher Jackson (October 8, 2020); 5.3 On Election Day, Vote for Candidates with Science-Based Policies, Not Politicians Who Ignore Evidence by the Editors of Scientific American (October 1, 2022); 5.4 More Scientists Need to Run for Office. This Advocacy Group Is Teaching Them How by Shaughnessy Naughton (October 26, 2022).

Each author biography was accurate at the time the article was originally published.

INDEX